CW00894208

A Funeral in Fiesole

Rosanne Dingli

Yellow Teapot Books
Australia

ISBN-13: 978-1519245779

ISBN-10: 1519245777

Yellow Teapot Books
Australia

Designed and typeset by
Ding! Author Services
Cover image and glyphs from
Fiesole near Florence in the Evening by TS Šimon (1877-1942)
Author portrait by Mark Flower

La lontananza sai è come il vento
spegne i fuochi piccoli
accende quelli grandi.

Domenico Modugno *La Lontananza*

Noi siamo duri come questa roccia.
Come questa pietra testardi.
E siamo accomodanti come la spuma del mare.

Concetta D'Orazio *Queste Pagine: Abbruzzo*

You know, distance is like the wind
It puts out small fires
And fans big ones.

Domenico Modugno *La Lontananza*

We are as hard as this rock.
Stubborn as this stone
And we are as compliant as the sea's foam.

Concetta D'Orazio *Queste Pagine: Abbruzzo*

Also by Rosanne Dingli

Death in Malta
Camera Obscura
According to Luke
The Hidden Auditorium
The White Lady of Marsaxlokk
How to Disappear

For more about this author visit
rosannedingli.com

I am grateful to my group of beta-readers, who helped improve initial drafts of this novel and made insightful suggestions. I also thank Concetta D'Orazio for kind permission to use verses from her writing. Help came from a dozen unexpected directions when I researched details to do with sailing, history, the geography of the Tuscan hills, cooking, and Italian art and music. I thank my family; they endure absentmindedness and more when I am writing, which is often.

A Funeral in Fiesole

Paola

Suzanna

Brod

Nigel

Paola

Wall gods

Back in the days of rattling bicycles, ice cream cones, and dog-eared comic books, it was summer here, all the time. Now it was wet and grey. I approached, hesitant in my little rental FIAT. I didn't know whether I would arrive first. I wanted to be first.

There were dead shrubs in oversized pots Mama placed along the driveway sometime back then, in my childhood; when we were all small. Brown twigs stuck out of them like fingers, darkened by a swift and sudden downpour in the last half-hour. Now fine drizzle blurred my windscreen and dampened my spirits as I drove unsteadily up the winding hills toward the inevitable, the unbearable.

I saw hope in a row of new trees – they resembled the pencil pines of the Melbourne suburb I so recently left, but could have been young cypresses – closer to the house and green, green.

Oh, those grey steps to the front door. We climbed them as children, and descended – down and up, up, down, up, shouting and laughing –

before and after so many family events. This one, this gathering here of all of us, was going to fill me with grief. It was still full of unknown prospects of the kind I did not like and always tried to avoid if possible. Not one for conflict, I strived all my life for personal compromise. I rarely battled for something I barely understood, and absolutely never for anything I sensed I could not win.

Uncertainty, conviction about an outcome – and often, not knowing the difference – was what held me back most of my adult life. So catching sight of the house as I sped up and parked the little white car, in the spot where as a child I would have pedalled cautiously along on a battered bike, made me think I was always somewhat reticent in coming forward to claim what was mine.

This occasion was of course no time to assert myself. Still, there was something I wanted. Now Mama was gone, I would have to find out whether it was in the house. Of course, I would have to seek a way to persuade the others it rightfully belonged to me. It would take some doing.

No geraniums, none of the brilliant flowers Mama liked along the driveway. Abandoned, the place appeared abandoned, wild. Decay showed itself at every turn. The glorious attention the house thrived in when we were young had ended. Awnings over the doors to the veranda were ripped and faded. Oh, the marble table out there was lopsided, lame on three curved metal legs, with only two wrought iron chairs left. Pushed in a corner, sodden and torn, lay something like an old beach umbrella. A caper bush grew out of a crack in the paving.

Mama stayed here almost until the end, quite as she had planned, brought all the way to be in this house when infirm, but it was obvious her capacity was greatly diminished. The staff, a faithful couple from Prato, was no longer there. It was a sad feeling. As for claiming what was mine – perhaps it was what we were all assembling for. All four of us clamouring for something with which to confirm the past, and affirm the present. Hah – and make the future more comfortable? Hopefully we did not clamour for the same things – but it was inevitable, in a way.

Knowing we would all arrive on the same day was good from one perspective, but I knew all the old stuff would be raked up, especially by those who thought they had a greater stake. It was silly to hope for the old place in its old glory; as futile as expecting everyone would say and do the right things.

Mama had her hopes for each of us. She knew me well, but I thought not as well as she deciphered the personalities, wishes, and claims of the others, who were more assertive, and demonstrative. As children, they learned how to make their feelings known, without a doubt. As adults, they chugged onward in their individual and combined forces. I often felt left out. Not singled out, but not as powerful as I had to be to counter their united dynamic vigour. This week, I needed to be forceful about something I wanted, and wanted rather badly, and Mama was not there anymore to hear me out.

'Paola!'

Someone called from the entry. Someone hidden, huddled inside out of the rain. I recognized the voice, and had to smile. I was not the earliest, then, nor the most eager, to get here. I turned my back to the house first, to summon my thoughts, to gauge my mood, to present a composed face to the others. Self-control they might recognize, even after my recent disasters and troubles. Even after the biggest surprise of my life. It was important to calm down, gather my wits, and carry myself like I arrived with good intentions. The scenery had that effect on me.

The more or less unchanged panorama had accompanied all my childhood woes and joys. Now it struck me, even in drenching rain, with the permanence of some things and the transience of most human deeds and concerns. Even the trees were the same ones I watched as a youngster, steadfast in the summer sun, or whipped sideways in some gale from the northeast in the fierce onset of autumn. I stood on 'our hill' and gazed down at the strange slender crenelated tower of the Fiesole cathedral through old eyes, and new eyes, at once. How foolish I was, to think anything about money, or words, or promises, or loans, or inheritance could transcend the longevity of trees and hills and houses. Yes, even houses, some houses, lived on without us, taking with them our stories, our bruised spirits, and our petty debacles.

'Hello, Paola! Isn't John with you?'

Reluctance to answer rose in my chest like heartburn. I climbed the wet treacherous stairs cautiously and with more doubt. It was a strong sense of unwillingness to enter a family reunion like no other we had ever had. My sister-in-law's voice was sophisticated but piercing, and I could detect a desire in her – even though we had not met eye-to-eye for a couple of years – to be hospitable. Harriet was welcoming me to my mother's house. Another person might have found this ironic, even in the circumstances.

We embraced in the Tuscan way, cordial and cool, warm and distant all at once. Graceful, Mama would have called our embrace and air kisses. Elegant.

'No – John's in Queensland, Harriet.' I was not about to spill stuff about John and me on the forecourt, in the rain. I did not want to muddy my entrance with the unpleasantness that had fouled my departure from Melbourne. 'But tell me first. How are you and Nigel?'

'Oh, Paola … you know… the children keep us on our toes.'

I sensed something cool there, apart from the chill resulting from a sharp telephone quarrel we had months before. Something kept Harriet and Nigel out of the first sentence she uttered about themselves. Mentioning the children was innocuous. Always safe.

'The gardens are looking a bit … ordinary.'

'In this rain, no wonder.' She saw it was not what I meant, but we both knew not to discuss the condition of the estate too much.

There were things about which we were not willing to talk yet. Urgent family things, which would inevitably spill out later. Private, personal things, which might bubble to the surface unbidden. Among siblings, siblings and their spouses, siblings and their children, little can remain hidden. Secrets have a habit of displaying themselves, artlessly, like a badly put-together dessert brought to table by a reluctant hostess who knows little about cooking, and less about guests.

I would soon discover, I supposed, the state of Nigel and Harriet's marriage, the real achievements or otherwise of their children, Lori and Tad. My niece and nephew, if and when they turned up, would demonstrate and remonstrate all they liked, but the true circumstances in which they lived and thrived would soon enough come to the fore.

Besides, I had matters of my own to keep to myself. There was also the issue I was to broach to them all. In truth, what I felt at that moment was the entire catastrophe of my life, a sodden fistful of regret. It had to wait ... until later, much later. If I could. If I could hold my tongue. 'Are Tad and Lori here?'

With perfect hands Harriet brushed imaginary rain from a shoulder. A new ring, I noted, with a tiny diamond, was a bit too loose for her finger, and trembled. Where was her lovely engagement ring?

'They'll be late. They're always running behind.' She paused. 'There are times I think stuff like that runs in families.' Her face changed slightly when she caught my eye. 'And at other times I shriek with laughter over the randomness of things.'

I smiled, widely, without the liveliness I was tacitly invited to share. Harriet shriek with laughter? She was holding back, and had little cheer herself. Little joyfulness was to be had in the chilly hallway. The faded but familiar frescoes were much more peeled and distressed than I remembered. Mould had added itself to the deterioration. Its damp choky smell seemed to cause the painted wall gods to grimace and shiver. How reassuring they were still there, though, one for each child, wielding their symbolism like family jokes no one else understood.

Ah – those wall gods.

Neptune was mine. I had claimed him long before the others took one each as well. I placed a damp hand on the wall near his leg. He fairly pushed through that faded red cape, gazing out at the viewer, squinting, as if he felt he was but an imperfect copy of the mural at Molina. But he was mine, and so were his watery henchmen in the stylized waves behind him. I often used to wish, as a lonely and dissatisfied child, for that trident. One tine in the eye for each of my siblings, and I would be alone, happy, fulfilled. Vicious thoughts, eventually transforming into the murder mysteries I wrote, which even today, such a long time after the first one was published, still sold well. Everyone thought I was this big literary success. No one knew my sorry little – big – secrets.

Diana the Huntress was of course Brod's. She was depicted sharply here – before the mould got her – with a quiver faded from once brilliant carmine, and hounds emerging from the ornate architrave of the door to the drawing room. Broderick naturally wanted Neptune. He always wanted what I had, including roller skates that did not fit him, and the set of *Girl's Own* annuals he pinched, one by one, from the box beneath my bed. Why he would want to read girls' stories was at the time unclear to me.

Further along the hall, I saw Apollo was the

best preserved of all the frescoes, most likely because of the heavy archway to the garden, or the fact he was Suzanna's god. On long summer afternoons, Suzanna and I would lie on the cool tiles and watch coloured rays from the stained glass window in the stairwell move along Apollo's bare torso. Yellow and green and ruby red. We would be called to dinner, and we'd hurry, flicking drops from hastily washed hands at the two boys.

Mars, clad only in a short mantle and metal helmet, faced Apollo across the red and white tiled space, where the central table always bore a tall vase of some variety of flowers from the garden. This was in the past a scratched and gouged table top; the repository for keys, purses, belts, wallets, books, and hotchpotch paraphernalia of our youth and childhood, so it was saddening to see it clear now, except for a thin layer of household dust and a large empty majolica bowl with chips the shape of fingernails in the wide brim.

Nigel's god, Mars – the reason Suzanna and I never wondered for a minute of our young days about male genitalia – frowned from under his gathered brow and peeling eyebrows. The morning sun got him regularly, so his original dark skin was bleached and pocked, and the powdery tideline of white mould got him at the knees. Someone said he was a less priapic copy of a Pompeiian Mars. His drunken shield lay abandoned underneath the row of our coat hooks, bare now apart from two jackets, where our holiday gear would hang. Nigel's god, he was, humourless and angry. As furious as Nigel could become when having too many siblings was too

8

much. He was the youngest, taking Mars because he was stuck with the last god.

Where was Nigel? Harriet had left me to myself in the hall, to park my wheeled case and hang up my coat, but I could still hear her thin voice somewhere inside, past the drawing room, whose rugs gave the impression of being damp and had started curling at the edges. I couldn't pause long enough to see whether what I wanted was in there. Past the dining room, where one of the chairs was missing. Someone had removed the fine lace curtains, leaving only heavy drapes pulled untidily to either side of each tall window in both the reception rooms. Because of the weather, everything seemed bathed in green and blue, in grey and a dull resistant brown in dark corners. I followed Harriet's voice to the kitchen.

'Paola!' Nigel stood at the stove, wooden spoon in hand. 'Flight okay? Tired?'

Before I could answer, Harriet said something about my old room. Without thinking, I stepped back to face her. 'Oh – of course I want my old room ... why ...?' I saw immediately how my words put her in charge. I bit my lip. Just because they were the ones doing the organizing when Mama was still alive, when they were looking after her, did not mean they were responsible now. Why *assign* me my own room?

'The ceiling's leaking. All this rain. We figured the roof space has to be saturated, for water to seep through the bedroom ceilings.' She imitated my lip biting.

I stared at her shoes, her hands, her hair. 'It always leaked a bit. Is it very bad?' I started towards the back stairs.

'Paola! You've hardly said hello. We'll see about bedrooms later. Brod will be here at seven, and Suzanna's coming with Lewis.'

Apologetic, I stepped back into the kitchen, which was warm and dry and as welcoming as it was all those years ago. Was it our old range, and could that possibly be the very same cavernous fridge of our childhood?

'Sorry, Nigel. It was a long drive. I'm all in a ... a blue funk.'

'Mama died, Paola. *Mama died*. It's to be expected. We'll all be better after the funeral.'

How could he know? 'Thank you for arranging everything.'

He straightened his mouth, lowered his eyes, surprised to find a wooden spoon in his hand. He placed it in a little puddle of tomato sauce on the counter. 'I'm making a mess.' He ripped a sheet of kitchen towel and swiped at the red smear, making it worse at first, and then managing to scoop and wipe it all off.

I watched, bewildered. The first mention of the funeral. I had by then been there a quarter-hour, considering the house, matching memories with the remnants of what once was.

'It wasn't as hard as I thought it might be. She ...' He wrestled with an enormous tea towel, and proceeded to fold it carefully, corner to exact corner. 'It was ... Paola, listen – she left written instructions. We knew what to do, the people to contact. Most things were previously paid for. We even know what music we are to play. Everything.'

'What music!' Surprised at Mama's final foresight, I moved back a step and leaned against the table, knowing it was there without having to look. Our big scarred heavy immovable kitchen table, whose top someone had once painted red. Its edge, its surface, its texture were so familiar to my hands I paused, realizing how easy it was to be thrown mentally, bodily, psychically, into the past.

'*Ombra mai fu*. Also, the Arvo Pärt piece, and other works ... you know.'

'The prelude from ...'

'Yes.' Nigel smiled, which pulled his eyes downward. 'Yes. All that.'

'And no Verdi Requiem.'

He laughed. 'No – no. *Ave verum corpus*, if there's time.' He pushed a mug of tea towards me.

'What!' Mama chose Mozart?

'Sit. Rest.'

It was starting to dawn on me that it would be hardest for Nigel. No. No – it would be most difficult for Brod.

'And no Palestrina.'

'Paola ...!'

'Okay. Okay. The twins and I will read at the service, I suppose?'

My little brother, my baby brother, now fifty-three, blinked. 'You're the oldest, Paola. Of course you'll read. We'll all read. Have you prepared anything? Suzanna and Brod don't have real choices.'

'Don't forget we have written directions.' Harriet came around the big table, pulled out a chair and sat lightly, gracefully, crossing long legs. 'The sauce, Nige.'

11

Her husband swivelled quickly and twisted a knob, which made the simmer subside. 'Have you noticed how hot tomato can get?'

'Suzanna and Brod can read ... the bit out of St Paul Mama liked, and the letter Papa ...'

'No! No letters. Too private. Not out of the dim distant past. Besides, we have her suggestions to choose from. She left a list.'

Harriet drummed perfect fingers on the scratched red tabletop. 'All right, Nige. Your father died when you were little children. He was out of ...'

'He was never *out of the picture*.' I was not about to let her tell me about my own father. 'I was fourteen, Harriet. Nigel was nine. The twins were eleven – eleven? – something of the sort. We all have good, live, vivid memories of ... of Papa.'

Nigel filled an enormous pot with water at a tap with a goose neck.

I changed the subject. 'When was *that* installed?'

Harriet tilted her head to see what it was I had noticed. 'Oh, the new taps. We had to have them put in when we lived here ... you know, all the plumbing essentially needs a good check. Taps were like, *urgent*.'

'Essentially?'

'Paola, please. Um ... no reading from a letter from Papa, then.' Nigel placed the pot on the stove and lit a flame. 'I feel I'm cooking for the entire population of Fiesole. How many will we be?' He started to count on his fingers. 'You and I. Paola. Suzanna and Lewis. Brod. Lori and ... Tad, perhaps.'

'Perhaps?'

Nigel lifted an eyebrow so pointed, and Harriet produced a sigh so loud, so protracted and dramatic, it was plain they were having issues with their son. I walked over to the fridge and pulled its old handle.

Inside, neatly arranged in categories, were obvious recent purchases intended to cater for a large crowd over a number of days. 'Is Brod bringing anyone?'

'It's not a party, Paola.'

I turned to my brother's wife. 'I know. It's a funeral. Is Brod seeing someone right now, I mean.'

'Grant. His name's Grant and he's an artist or something.' She seemed pleased there was something I didn't know. Filling me in was a pleasure. I could see it in her eyes. She continued with a bit less dryness in her tone. 'We've never met him, but they've ... it's been a year or more, on and off.'

'Goodness – a year?'

'He said he and Grant would stay down at the *Ponte Guisto*, even though I said they'd be welcome to his old room.' Harriet's sharp statement was more potent than the aroma from Nigel's sauce pot.

It was evidently because she put it like she did that Brod refused her vicarious hospitality. Her proprietary way. Her ownership of all that was ours. She stood and shook out a brightly coloured checked tablecloth over the round table.

'We're not eating in here?'

'Why not, Paola?' Her black hair curtained one side of her face when she raised her eyes. 'It's only family.' She straightened her back. And her mouth. 'I said only a minute ago it's not a party.'

Nigel

Noise and disruption

We ended up eating in the big dining room, of course. The fact Paola thought it was silly to eat in the kitchen got on my nerves, but I think I managed to hide it. Harriet, patient and calm, unfolded another tablecloth, a rectangle of threadbare white damask, which had not been used in years, and draped it over a third of the long dining table. So we all pushed together at the end closest to the door to the passage and the kitchen.

They all found fault with everything. Well, almost. It was mostly Paola. I put up with it, like I always did, and smiled, smiled, smiled, even with the smell of garlic still on my fingers. Even with Paola examining all our expressions. She was so transparent. She was so ruthlessly calculating. She was waiting for an opportunity to say something momentous. It was there in her eyes. Sad, sad eyes, but with sharpness in them I recognized. She was after something.

'We could have eaten in the kitchen, you know.'

'This place is falling to pieces.'

'It's so cold in here.'

'Where are the lace curtains?'

'Is that the garden door slamming?'

'What, no red wine?'

'Mama would have used the good cutlery.'

Later, someone praised the food, which made Harriet smile. I knew her cooking secrets and shortcuts, and often copied them. She could be quick and efficient, and clean and everything, but she cut corners with recipes, used packets and pouches to boost her flavours and sauces, so some of it was faux. Still, she believed in spending time with people rather than chopping-boards, as she so funnily expressed her lack of desire to spend too much time standing at a counter with a sharp knife in hand. Well, I thought she was funny, but I doubt my oldest sister ever found my wife the least bit amusing.

Paola helped to carry out crockery and glasses, stopping from time to time to study our body language, our expressions, what we were wearing, and paused meaningfully at the end of some of our sentences. She weighed and measured everything in her head, my eldest sister, and could not wait, it was obvious, for the twins and their respective partners to arrive.

But it was our daughter who got there first, running around from the servants' quarters at the back. Damp from the rain even from the brief dash from the garden, Lori chose her words, as I expected.

She was reticent and patient with the whole *Gramma's funeral* thing, and restricted what she said to pleasantries and small talk. My children were fascinating to Paola. As the only nephew and niece in the family, it was no wonder.

'I left the cello in the back house. I'll bring it up when it's stopped raining. I guess you guys won't mind if I play, but I'm setting down a new piece for the festival. Luckily it's here. The timing is excellent.'

I raised an eyebrow at my daughter, without a word. I slid meaningful eyes toward her aunt Paola.

Lori responded immediately. 'Oh – I know. Funerals are hardly expected to fit around other events, but it so happens we're playing at the *Maggio Musicale*, in Florence.'

Harriet beamed.

Paola would see pride in her eyes, even past my wife's long black hair. I waited for my sister to say something about playing, or instruments, or music. Or even the funeral. She simply examined Lori with those impassive eyes. Blank eyes which did not quite hide the sentiments and thoughts written into the lines on her face. She was approaching the last years of her fifties, and could still not completely mask her reactions and feelings. It was plain envy I saw there. I could see she wondered how she would have raised a daughter of her own.

I doubted Paola had ever been present to hear Lori's cello in the house. She cocked her head to catch sounds of another arrival in the hall. We all heard keys and things thrown onto the table, and Brod's high voice.

He entered the dining room talking. '... and

16

here you all are! Hello, hello. Paola – good drive? Nice flight?' He inclined his head at Harriet and me. 'Hello Nige ... hello, hello.' He put his head back out through the hall door and called. 'Come in, Grant, for heaven's sake.' His smile was so broad it widened his long face at the mouth in a cartoonesque way. The moustache – something new – did not help. 'Grant?' Breathless, he was, and very nervous, for a reason we all guessed. 'Paola – have you and Grant ever met?'

Introductions, explanations, recounts of their drive. Paola's reaction to Grant's appearance was predictable. Handsome, too handsome, he gave the impression he should be on the big screen, or on the stage, or a model at the very least. Nothing like it. Grant was an architectural draftsman, or engineer, or designer, or something; arresting grey eyes and all. What he ever saw in Brod – well, it was obviously Brod's wit and slap-dash ways ... so very attractive and winning. Possibly the only gregarious soul in the family. No, no – Suzanna was our extrovert. There was also his caring personality, a feminine sympathy we all earlier on thought was part of being a twin. The empathy of being half of something, we all thought, before we could guess. Mama grasped it immediately. For Mama, things tended to fall into place when they happened, even if they were a shot out of the blue.

I remembered how Paola took Brod's sexuality the first time he walked in with an obviously camp university boyfriend. Chilly, she was; aloof and supercilious. Analytical more than accepting. So many years ago, before she left for Australia. She went off so young. Where had all those years gone?

Harriet had to get used to my strange family from the start, I supposed. From my mother who was an heiress, who painted a little, whose money allowed her many mistakes and privileges, and much enviable leisure. Mama, with her small house in Cornwall and a sizeable villa in Tuscany. This predictable summer house, where we spent all school holidays in a warm cultural sun-bath. Yes, from Mama, to all four of us siblings.

We grew up half Italian simply because of where we lived our summers. My wife never met our father, of course. We four all had different, if vague, memories of his attempts at opening small cafés and bistros. Abandoning projects through premature sales; he did that a lot. Once or twice he surprisingly made more money than anyone ever imagined. The stuff of family legend.

Paola, because of her age, remembered more than any of us about Papa's misguided forays into the hospitality industry. Even renovating this house with the view of turning it into a B & B was part of his whole energetic idea-driven exploits.

Mama had easily laughed it off. 'Do you think we could have guests among the children's mess and noise all summer, darling?' Her calm amused question, at the time Papa was thinking of applying for permits and things, stopped everything in its tracks.

He came to see she would never cooperate. That was when he saw it for the first time; or so Paola tells it. Evidence remains of his efforts. Some of the bigger bedrooms up in the far wing were redone.

And now here we were, all coming together for

Mama's funeral. All wondering when the conversations – for now so superficial and cordial – would come down to the greedy. Paola, and her use of complicated vocabulary, would say the *pecuniary*, the *acquisitive*. My older sister uses words like weapons, and her face betrays her emotional state when she does. Her lean frame and her short primly parted dark hair loudly announced her methodical personality.

If only we, Harriet and I, could be choosey – about words or feelings. We had no choices. We needed money, and we needed it fast. Frankly, we had put so much towards caring for Mama we deserved at least as much as a quarter of everything.

Losing my job in the spring was something we never bargained for. How could I, such a competent programmer, suddenly find myself unemployed at fifty-three, with apparently little prospect of finding anything else immediately to provide the all-important income? How could Harriet cope? Realistically speaking, her work never made enough for anything else apart from the upkeep of our cars and the expenses of two rather demanding children and their high maintenance lives; musical instruments and all that. We were getting deeper in debt with each passing week. The mortgage on our London flat was eating us alive.

Being the youngest meant I had to be most generous with time and money to Mama. Well – Harriet had not always thought so, but her sarcastic flippancy was something I could take. She came around in the end. We spent time and a lot of money moving Mama from the Cornwall house to this crumbling place because she said for months she wanted to die here.

She died in hospital after all, a full ten months after the move, most of which time she spent in a home; and although one cannot with any confidence say a Tuscan hospice is the same as an English one, she could not have known the difference during those last few weeks. The last four days were packed with confusion and sorrow I could hardly stand. On top of it all, I was the only one of the children here to endure it. The only one. I would never forget it.

Now, we gathered in the old house, several numb days later, for the very important funeral. Harriet made some very pointed remarks to me in private about my siblings' headlong rush to Fiesole, simply to hear the will read, but I understood Harriet very well. She expressed grief in a funny way. She always seemed closer to Mama than my own sisters.

There, I thought it, even if I never said it. Mama loved Harriet for her clever cynicism, her way with a sharp sentence. Her efficiency, too. My wife had a special frugality with time and money Mama understood, even if she could not practice it herself. Harriet was acutely aware of our precarious finances, and was as anxious as I was to find out how the contents of the will would change our fortunes.

There was Suzanna's entrance. Late, noisy, disruptive, like she always was. You could never tell she was half of something, unlike with Brod, who was so easily seen by everyone to be her twin. She was unique – insistently so – and made it a point to stay that way. If Papa had lived, she would have been his foil. It was what Mama always said about

Suzanna. 'My business-minded daughter ... such an entrepreneuse!' With the difference, of course, that her schemes and plans worked. She saw things through, unlike Papa. But then, she had Lewis.

Lewis, the model husband. He came in behind her, carrying their bags straight into the dining room, where we were all sitting, before I had time to bring in the large platter. The commotion was tremendous. I stood at the doorway and waited, debating whether to slide everything in the oven to keep it warm. Luckily, it was a gelid kind of day, and the salad in the glass bowl on the round table would not wilt.

'There you all are, already! How clever to get here before us! Driving up our hill was something in the rain! Listen everybody – we've done it! Haven't we, Lewis? We sold the new franchise!' Her acknowledgments were breezy, staccato. Suzanna always spoke in exclamations. Always about her own affairs first. Something that would have seemed selfish to an outsider. Grant watched her with curious eyes.

If she were a writer like Paola, Suzanna would have run out of exclamation marks a long time ago. 'Everything's settled! We got what we asked, or very nearly precisely. Now we can buy a new boat! Can't we, Lewis?'

Lewis's mild lopsided smiles went around, face to face to face, then he pulled a chair up for himself at the distant unclothed end, hidden by the tarnished silver centrepiece. His salutations were hardly audible. This was a man who longed to disappear at the earliest opportunity. A man more at home with spreadsheets, with organizing our sister's life, than with conversation.

His wife was belatedly hugging her twin. Lewis watched from behind the silver epergne, obviously not the only one to be struck once more by the similarities in her appearance and Brod's. His collar-length hair, his dark blue eyes, his mouth crammed with teeth, his large ears; they were all repeated identically in Suzanna, who managed – with expert make-up and a gifted hairdresser – to turn the dubious features into assets. She oozed style, even after a long drive in the rain. The tiny dog under her arm was as mute and awe-struck as her husband, who hid behind the centrepiece and waited for the chance to escape. Did he hate all company, or was it only this family that set his teeth so on edge he could hardly speak?

'So ... so sad about Mama, hmm? We can't get over it! Can we, Lewis?' She sat in my chair, removed a scarf, plonked the little dog in her lap so its snout came to rest on the table, and sighed audibly. 'I guess you guys have made all the arrangements. I saw the announcements in the papers. Anyone thought of the service ... and things?'

'I emailed you, Suzanna.'

She lifted her chin at me. 'Oh yes, Nigel. You know me and my memory!'

She had perfectly good recall. But the others were talking, so she shifted her attention to what was going on in the room, and I was left to organize it so Lewis joined us on the tablecloth, so dinner was served hot, and that there was enough to drink.

Someone asked, above the chatter, where Tad

was. My son was always late, and meeting the uncles and aunts, preparing for *Gramma's funeral*, the hubbub of having everyone in the house was not Tad's idea of an enjoyable time. He would most probably saunter in, unobtrusive, simmering with something he never spoke about, after dinner, when everyone's overtures had been well and truly sung.

Suzanna

Ruthless and blunt?

What a fuss they all made, when we were only an hour late! Lewis was driving, so we had to take our time, and taking the ring road around Florence in the rain was not his idea of a fun drive. On top of it all, Otto needed a pit-stop or two.

'Not again!' Lewis loves the dog, but occasionally forgets he is a live and sentient being with needs and desires similar to ours. Poor Otto – he has to put up with Lewis's concept of what's right and proper, even when it comes to toilet stops on a very long drive in Italian traffic. A very long drive from the ferry, for Mama's funeral in Fiesole. She died less than a fortnight ago, and I'm only now used to the idea she is no longer there. No longer pottering about in the garden of the old villa, no longer arranging flowers on the round hall table, watched by our wall gods.

How drab and decrepit those murals had become! Someone should have had them painted over in some nice pearl grey paint, long ago. The whole house needed a facelift. It was nothing – nothing – compared to the cosy little house in Cornwall. These gardens were awful, and the whole place smelled of mildew and mould.

On one side of the hall, the stairs spiralled upward, taking the frescoes upstairs to the landing. I remembered my little fingers tracing each ruined floral twist, each faded and flaking sprig of leaves, each washed-out hidden bird and all the peeling detaching snails and insects the forgotten artist worked into the grand design. Oh, it was grand once, but I looked and looked, and found nothing worth saving. The worn little birds in the foliage all along the bottom, in the frieze of climbing roses, were crumbling away. White, crimson, salmon pink birds, whose painted colours turned, over the years of my childhood, to paler versions of themselves, with feathers yellowing. They would never ever take flight.

Paola, sentimental Paola, thought they were constant, perpetual, like Donato and Matilde, who attended to the place – and us – every summer of our lives. Well – painting over the semi-perpetual birds would not be such a great loss. The motionlessness of a mural was nothing like the loyalty of servants. They cared for us and spoiled us, watching us grow. We used to wonder, as children, what they did during the winter when we were at school, and when Mama was in Cornwall.

'Mama – where do Donato and Matilde fly to in the winter, when we fly back to school?'

'They're not migratory birds, my darling. They stay in Fiesole.'

I was a bird! So we were migratory birds, and always had Christmas in Cornwall. A red and green and silver Christmas with very few variations. Also, we forgot all about our caretakers in Fiesole until the following June, when we descended upon the big echoing house. A noisy crowd of four, all tumbling out of the big car and up those grey stone steps to the front door, shouting and running up and down!

'Where are the skates I left behind?'

'Oh – see? My orange cardigan is still on a hook!'

'There's a new cat, did you notice?'

'I wish Donato would hurry with the bags!'

'I'm hungry. When is lunch?'

And Mama, who had been there for days before our arrival from boarding school in England, would come down the stairs with arms outstretched, like she had been waiting forever. They had bought the villa for a song, when Papa was still alive. Oh, Papa! He dreamed of turning it into a *pensione*, with celebrities arriving for what he termed sojourns.

It never happened, of course. We were far too noisy and messy as children. Besides, we took up a lot of room, four of us. The boys had the two back bedrooms at the end of the wing, on either side of the passage, one facing the view over Florence, and the other the back dip in the hills, with the church spires bursting through the rooftops like toothpicks on a tray of cheese. The boys did not care for views.

Paola and I had two rooms with a central bathroom closer to the main bedrooms on the grand landing, where the ornate grandfather clock ticked away the interminable minutes of our childhood and youth. How we fought! That bathroom was a battlefield – my jumbled stuff and damp towels, and her obsessively neat rows of bottles and tubes and boxes and brushes and jars and things!

She was always observant and quiet, and I was always bursting with energy. She could have been different if she wanted. She could have teased Papa about his clock too!

Paola was not the only one with memories. Mine were of Papa, and how close we were. How well I remembered opening the beautifully carved door of that clock, holding the pendulum still for a while, releasing it and setting it swinging again, about a minute slow! Papa would eventually notice and set it right, checking it against his accurate wristwatch with the brown strap, which Mama said he bought in Switzerland, on their honeymoon.

He would take me on his lap and explain how there was advantage in keeping good time, how wonderful it was to have such an accurate clock, and how there was snow on Swiss mountains even in June. Also, how there was no sea in Switzerland; something I could only imagine if I tried very hard. So how did they sail their yachts? Papa would laugh, and go on to talk of lakes, and sails, and wooden boats.

What stories, what memories we all had to share! Some of them admittedly happy, in my opinion, but most collapsing, like the balustrades on the balconies outside the windows of the upstairs sitting room. Fading, like the garlands of raised plaster flowers on the double doors up there. The place was crumbling to the ground!

'Nothing, but nothing, is nicer than a grand Italian villa furnished in the English way,' Mama would say, to anyone who would listen. She brought furniture and fittings out in crates from Cornwall, and took a lot of enjoyment decorating the house and arranging the gardens. I liked the furniture. It was the only thing I loved. Solid English furniture. It lasted. It did not date, and was always stylish, always. English furniture made me happy.

Oh, what sadness was to come! But the grief when Papa died did not touch Fiesole. He went to heaven from Cornwall, Mama would say. He rose from the dinner table one night, clutching his chest, and never sat there again. The story broke my heart, every time it was told.

We were all at school, even 'little Nigel' who had just started along with Brod, and who took to being a boarder at St Clements without batting an eyelid. I remember the fuss Brod had made – tears and tantrums and more tears! – but it was because I could not go to the same school as he, and we were very close twins. Inseparable, at ten years old.

And now we were all here, waiting, waiting, for something to happen, getting on each other's nerves in the same way as we started doing the instant Paola turned twenty and it was about time, she said, that we all went our separate ways and did not bother to return to Fiesole for the holidays. Her suggestion hurt Mama, I do remember the expression in her eyes.

Paola did not come the following summer, and

neither did Nigel, thinking we would all stay away. Brod and I came, of course, and cheered Mama up, while we helped her plant what seemed like several thousand bulbs among the trees at the back! Wonderful. I could not remember now what they were; gladioli? Daffodils? Irises? I had no clue! It would be nice to walk out there later with Otto, and see how time obliterated everything she did.

How time changed us! Brod had grey hairs. Thank goodness my hairdresser was so good and so affordable. I would hate to think my forehead was as corrugated as his. They were happy corrugations, Nigel said. Happy! He wasn't always. Brod was happy now, with Grant. Could he be, at last?

Having a gay twin made one wonder about oneself. What if I were a boy – what if we'd emerged from the same sac? I often wondered what it would be like to be identical rather than fraternal. It would either have made me male and gay; or Brod female and ... and whimsical. Lewis called me capricious, which was something I could not agree with. How could I be capricious, in business? I thought he used the word instead of cold. Instead of ruthless. He regarded me so strangely when I went ahead and took Carmody & Beck to court. Perhaps Lewis thought me heartless. Well, I might very well appear to be – but I won, and came away with a settlement that gave me more than half the deposit on my next investment. Capricious!

Papa did not think me whimsical. He knew I was the only one he could teach how to sail; the only one who would join him on the spotless deck of his boat in Cornwall. It might have been winter, but I was always there, listening to him talk about treacherous tides. He taught me my knots, how to turn a winch, and to 'feel the wind' by closing my eyes and turning my face to it. I learned how to find the wind's direction before I was seven.

'Suzanna, look – I've tied a short length of yarn to this shroud. What's it for, do you think?'

'To see how the breeze is blowing, Papa! I can tell from the way it flutters.'

'Good girl. A sailor's life revolves ...'

'... around the wind!'

He would smile and light another cigarette. 'And that's a fact.'

I would have liked this family to face a few facts. Not by being capricious, but by being blunt. Realistic! All my siblings were adults – goodness! Nigel was the baby at fifty-three. We had all been through hell at some point. Now was the time to gather our wits, break with the past, sell both Mama's old crumbling properties, and do something worthwhile with any money we could get.

Brod would agree, if I gave him a dig in the ribs. Hah! An elbow in the side from me got him out of the clutches of a jealous possessive boyfriend a few years ago. It was a similar dig – even though given on the phone – which motivated him to take a very lucrative job a few summers ago, which he still had. He never thanked me, but he came to me for advice! He did. Brod would never admit it, but he did.

Nigel and Harriet always talked, talked, talked things over until neither of them could make their minds up about what to do about anything. It took them months to resolve to care for Mama. When they finally did, though, they went the distance, even bringing her here from Cornwall, which must have been difficult in all senses of the word. Money! Time! Their own affairs had to go on hold for a while, and the children had to be patient. Patient and resentful, in all likelihood.

Well, everyone says Tad and Lori are great kids. Still, they weren't always. I used to doubt the effectiveness of raising kids the way Nigel and Harriet did it. The outcome – I had to admit – was not so terrible.

What to do about Paola was the biggest hurdle. She always dug her heels in, always examined everyone with those impassive eyes, always calculated everything mathematically and precisely, and quietly disapproved of everything. We were going to have to combine forces to persuade our big sister to sell this old pile.

The murals, the crumbling masonry, the moisture stains on all the ceilings. The pervading horrible mildew smell!

Brod

Potential in the rain

Bringing Grant to my mother's funeral irked Nigel's wife, even if she knew we had been together a year. Harriet is a bit like my eldest sister Paola, a person so infinitely easy to annoy, even if one tried hard not to do it. Harriet was so annoyed to find Grant so good-looking. I expected her to come out with an inane observation such as, 'The boys always get the longest eyelashes.'

She also reacted like a straight man – no wonder she and Nigel were so well suited to each other. They both seemed irritated, again, by Grant's ability to keep calm and cordial no matter what was going on. Not a brooding silence; no, it was not his way at all. It was calm anticipation something would happen, either to release him from a situation, or to present a general improvement of things. Patience for change. Something that drew me and my impulsiveness to him.

They always called me impulsive and rebellious, and I guess I behaved as they expected. I made sure I did. Late in life, I found someone who told me I didn't have to. A touch too late, for some things.

Grant always said, 'Change comes, Brod. You can't stop change. You don't have to push anything with such force.' And he was always right.

Even when I said I could not stay in the house. It was much too painful for me. All the holidays here with Mama. All the fights with Papa. It was Mama's absence I could not bear to ignore, or let go. Or abandon the possibility of meeting her, in her dirty gardening gloves and fraying straw hat, banging her feet on the side door grating and mat, grumbling at the amount of soil she would track into the passage behind the kitchen. Pushing a broom before her over the old tiled floor; an impatient Don Quixote tilting a domestic lance.

I could not possibly take it.

'Okay – we'll stay in Florence or something,' he said. 'Easy.'

And it was.

I could not bear to walk around the side bedrooms without hearing her walk up to my door, tapping with a knuckle. 'Brod, I made pancakes.' It was impossible to stay there, sleep there, wake up in the morning knowing Mama was not downstairs, fighting with the coffee filter machine. It was like being seventeen all over again; but if I examined this closely enough – had I ever grown out of the mixed up, juvenile stage?

I fought it – I struggled with it all my life. A

rebellion so strong I went into banking, of all staid and steady things. Lucrative, but not special. It was the type of career that was more successful than I needed it to be. Entirely the trajectory I was not expected to take, took anyway, and excelled at, to my own detriment. There was no excitement in my life. I spited myself, a kind of mock rebellion, which I could do nothing to fix, now I was in my fifties.

Mama might have felt it. I could not possibly walk around the grounds and not return to being a child again, a teenager again; spotting some project of hers, finished or not, or the way she got all the bulbs mixed up before they were planted among the trees, resulting in a higgledy-piggledy jumble of irises, daffodils, crocus, jonquils, and gladioli the following year. How she laughed. I could have been like that too, but I fought it. I battled with it all.

I wasn't here when she died, and I'll never forgive myself. How could I be here? It was such a sudden announcement from Nigel, on the phone. I anticipated what he would say and tried to stop him. I didn't want to hear the words *Mama's dying*. She was weak and frail and befuddled the last time I was with her, holding her hand in the hospice, but when Nigel phoned, and I picked up in the middle of an important conference in New York, I imagined her as she was when we all jumped out of the car at holiday time, when Donato drove us up to the house and we spilled out, quarrelling, laughing, loud and childish, with our gear, onto the gravel at the front, and ran up the grey steps to her widespread arms.

I had a terrible time at boarding school, and Nigel was no help because he was the archetypical perfect schoolboy, a star scholar with no hurdles and obstacles to do with his sexuality. He was younger, but he was everything I could not be. I was never the older, perfect Larkin boy. I was a startling comparison, a Larkin let-down. Always an eleventh-hour essayist, with permanent confusion in my heart about some fifth or sixth former with perfect teeth. Always enamoured of some drawling voice in the low register that struck at one's stomach, and a particular adolescent male ability to shoot glances that killed one on the spot.

I died many times before sixth form, and finally fell into the predatory arms of Fletcher Blancbaston – he with the medieval name and the medieval cheekbones, who signified wealth to the teachers and headmaster; he who could get away with anything because of the way he tossed his over-long hair. Through him I learned many things about myself, about other boys, and about gender confusion. About denial and rebellion.

'You're too soppy, Broderick Larkin – it's what's wrong with you,' he said once in his alarming voice. He climbed back into his pants and smiled so disarmingly it negated his harsh words for years before I saw true meaning in them. 'Don't be such a nancy. Stand up for yourself and wear the pants *for gossake*. Only idiots will want you to girl it around, asking for abuse, asking for your heart to be broken. Stand up for yourself and be a gay *man*.'

I thought at the time he was getting at me for being young. It took a few years before I found my style, my way of being, and a couple of decent guys. I think it was only because of Mama.

There was a place on the back stairs where she and I collided once – what was I, seventeen? – and it was a bit of a dance because she was carrying a big tray laden with a lemonade jug and many stacked glasses. I yelped and stood out of the way, and she stopped.

'Brod, take this tray from me. Will you manage?'

And in that ebullient holiday mood, I said, 'I can manage anything, Mama!'

Her face grew serious. 'Good. Do it. Be yourself. Manage it. Don't try to pretend anything else. Don't fight stuff all the time. Some things simply are. I know how you feel. I know who you are, all right, Brod? And it's ...' She smiled so brightly and seemed so proud and accepting of me the tray very nearly slipped out of her hands and mine. 'Ooops. There, got it?'

I got it. I got more than not smashing a tray full of glasses. I understood she accepted the fact I was queer, and she didn't mind one bit. I didn't have to hide or fight it. It was the most revealing summer of my life.

And now this place was empty. Empty. Everyone was here, but it was empty because Mama was gone. I took Grant down the back way to try and lay her ghost, but she was there. 'Come, I'll show you something.'

Grant followed me all the way down the back way, where the light was dull because of the high windows, to the back steps. 'What?'

She was there, dusting garden soil from her hands, eyes twinkling, head nodding, ever the optimist. In a way, she was a bit like Grant. Positive, knowing a positive change would eventually come. All one had to do was wait ... and not fight.

'Look – this was where I'd read and do stuff in the holidays.' The lump in my throat was enormous. I pointed around the oddly-shaped room. She was there; her chair, her tapestry stool, her shelf of gardening books and seed catalogues, but I did not mention the feeling to Grant.

'Oh – a cellar.'

'Not a basement, wait. Well, yes and no.' We moved further into the room and there were the wide glass doors with the back view of the hills, and the bumpy mountains in the distance, all purple and black in the rain. 'See? The house is built into the hill, see? Our hill, we call it. So there are views on each side, and stairs and steps in odd places.'

'It's enormous, Brod. Why are we staying in the village, or whatever it is? Why did we book a room? Everyone's so ...'

'Welcoming?' I laughed. I knew he'd soon see how my siblings were.

We stared out at the damp landscape together, and I thought how Mama often came down there to sit in the big brown chair to get away from what was happening in the house and catch her breath. I'd come down too. We wouldn't talk. We would ignore each other and listen to each other's breathing, and take in the view. It was like I heard her thoughts then. She would always know the first rain would come when it was time for us all to head back to school. She would stay and rest a few days longer, after we were all packed off, and eventually head to winter in Cornwall.

'So what's down there?'

'If it weren't raining so hard I'd take you down those steps – they're cut into the bank, see? – and descend to the next terrace. It's a bit of lawn surrounded by large pots, flower borders, you know the sort of thing. It's the ideal place for a pool, you'll see that for yourself – but we never had one.'

I had sat on the steps down there with Mama summer after summer, and talked about how glorious it might be to have a pool right on that grassed terrace. She would get me to pace it out; seven metres one way, four metres the other way. *Perfect*, we would say together, knowing it was a dream. Since Papa died she had to be careful. Her own mortality must always have been on her mind, not knowing she would live into her eighties. Knowing her caution was simply that. We feasibly could have had the pool. I didn't think it ever was money that stopped her.

I wondered about her last days at the hospital. Nigel and Harriet wouldn't say much. It would have had to be harrowing for Nigel. Harriet too. Mama loved her in a way, and one could not know someone for years on end and not be saddened by their death.

One expected to find Donato and Matilde here too. They were part of the furniture and we grew up with them in the background. Donato fixed things, even bandaged knees with the same patience he would lag a hot-water pipe. He could do a lot with his funny cloth bag of tools and wooden folding ladder, which seemed part of him. Donato wasn't Donato without his paint-stained ladder.

Matilde fixed everything else with pasta, pieces of cheese, her pickled olives, and those magical *cantuccini* baked from a recipe from her home town of Prato. 'Make no mistake, Broderick. These are Prato biscuits, and they have conquered the world.' Oh, that accent. Her clear Florentine dialect, which we all got to patter in by the time we grew to teenage.

Matilde was right. I remember dunking her biscuits into milky coffee in a bowl. I remember the big red round table and how she would wring out a dishcloth and vigorously rub it all clean while I sat there eating. The squeak of the cloth, the smell of yellow soap, the presence of someone silent there, active but silent, doing things around me; it all still made the hairs on the back of my neck prickle. I thought I learned about pleasure, and from where it can come, and the unexpected things that give pleasure, in that kitchen.

I could tell Grant fell in love with the house. Not only its size. 'It's massive, Brod. It's more than big – it's absolutely lovely. Where does the passage behind us lead?'

I took him up and back down the vaulted corridor and we ascended the back stairs to the wing, where some of the rooms were renovated. Papa's B & B plans, schemes, and dreams never came true, but a lot of work and expense had gone into the house. Mama admired some of the improvements. The rooms down this way were smaller than the bedchambers upstairs in the main block of the mansion, but they were pretty.

'It's because this part of the house was built

39

much later, I think. Successive owners added, took away, renovated ... you know.'

Grant walked on. 'It's what's so lovely about it. I like organic houses where the changes happen through the years, where you can see the pauses and the re-takes. There's nothing more maddening than a house all built and decorated to one instant plan.' He opened double doors and peeked into a bedroom whose walls were butter yellow. Even on a dull rainy day it was a bright sunny room. Even with an English ticking mattress rolled up on a metal bed base, curtains hanging to an expedient knot in their ends, and crates of things piled in corners; even with a door standing ajar showing a dated bathroom, it was attractive. I saw it too.

'What's happening to the house, Brod? It's not being sold, is it? It would be such a shame.'

I could see what he was thinking. 'I could never afford to buy Suzanna, Paola, and Nigel out, Grant – it can't happen.'

'Would a mortgage ...? Would ...? No, I guess not, but it would be wonderful if it stayed in the family so we could visit. Can you see us in this yellow room, eh, can you?' He smiled, charming, his beautiful face twisted into a playful grimace.

'I can. What we should do is talk Paola into buying us out – our share at least. Paola is most likely the only one who can afford it ... she's an author. I told you.'

'I thought Suzanna and Lewis ...'

'They're buying an enormous yacht. Their heart is set on it. It can only be Paola, my sister the author.'

'Not a household name author, though.'

'No – but she's written something like ... what? Thirty mystery novels? Paola Larkin, and her special detective, Emanuele Bondin. It should mean something – she does sell books. How do we get her to buy us out? I'd rather she had it than either of the others. Oh – look, it'll never happen.' I walked to the next double doors and opened them to reveal a small bedroom whose walls were a shade of rust. The ceiling cornice was decorative, and there were French windows to a small balcony, drenched with rain. The balustrade out there was not safe. 'It would take a fortune to fix the place, Grant. Even you can see it.'

'Especially me. I have to stop myself doing sums in my head. Take me away. Take me away! I'm thinking of how we could have this place.'

'We can't.'

'I know – we can't.'

'You still want it, though.'

'Of course I do. I'd give my right arm.'

I wondered how Mama felt when she was still here, what she put in her will, and whether it would present problems for us. Would she have left this crumbling Tuscan mansion to us all, to quarrel over? And what about the cottage in Cornwall?

Grant read my mind. 'There's a house in England too, isn't there?'

'Yes – but it's small, with only four bedrooms, only two bathrooms. Nothing like this.'

He laughed. 'Only four bedrooms.' He thought we were all privileged spoilt kids, even though we were all now in our fifties. 'What's it like, the one in Cornwall?'

'It overlooks the estuary, in Newquay, a funny place with extra bedrooms built into the roof space. Nigel and I had to share. We all crammed into it at Christmas, and Mama decorated everything with silver. Silver tree, silver ornaments, silver tinsel ... you know.'

'You loved it.'

'Yes. Paola didn't. She thought Christmas was a waste of time and she hated the cold. She hated the church thing.'

'Church!'

I laughed. 'Mama liked the traditional, the festive ... I don't know ... the ceremonial thing about Christmas. She didn't go to church otherwise, we were never religious or anything, but we'd all jump into our best gear and go to a Christmas service and sing.'

Grant's eyes showed something like pleasure, or like envy. 'My childhood was nothing like yours.'

'We didn't all want it. We didn't all enjoy it every year. We had nuts and oranges and this huge pudding Papa would set aflame when we were quite little. Nigel wanted to do it when he died, but the job fell to me because I was older.'

Grant dug his chin into my shoulder. 'You set a pudding aflame.'

'Mm.'

'Such a jolly family. Didn't you ever fight or anything?'

I had to laugh again. 'Continually. I always wanted what Paola had. She was secretive and cagey. Selfish. I stole comics and books from her room, and she would chase me down the stairs flicking a wet towel at my legs.'

'Girls' comics. How very Brod.'

'Yes. Well, the stories made more sense than Dennis the Menace and Desperate Dan.'

Paola

A mistake to look backward

The funeral was on the coming Saturday, which meant many more unsettling nights in my old room. I always had the same dreams in this house, identical to the ones I had as a teenager. Brod and Grant did the right thing by staying in town. Who wanted to lie awake waiting for drops from the ceiling to ding and splash into a zinc bucket on the rug?

I didn't want to gaze at Neptune on the wall, on the way up. He would squint at me, to say, 'You'll never have it your way. You'll never persuade anyone about anything.'

And yet, and yet, I wanted the house more than I wanted anything. No – there was one more thing, which might be impossible to find – lost forever. Everything was lost.

Last night, I sat up, startled by the sound of rain against my window panes, and wished for the thick insulating curtains and shutters on my wonderful Melbourne house. My dream-come-true house. I made sure everything in it was perfect before John and I moved there from our first home, and we undertook two thorough renovations through the years. I promised myself the perfect office, to write in. When the contract and advance for my third series came in, I was fortunate enough to get it. More time has been spent in my office than in any other room.

Living close to the sea in Melbourne was not unlike Cornwall used to be, John would insist. We had spent enough time in the Newquay cottage for him to make a good comparison. It was different for me of course. He did not have a childhood like mine, with Mama insisting on a traditional Christmas dinner, and a traditional this and a traditional that. I would resent it as a thirteen year-old. Now, I saw how it had shaped and formed me. Could it be I was starting to take on Mama's conventional ways?

John grew up in Australia, where everything was pleasantly back-to-front, with scorching Christmases and large platters of prawns, and bodysurfing on white beaches until his skin was pink and wrinkly. The surfing was why he liked Newquay. The fact it had a nice square tower, like the one in Fiesole, meant little to him. He didn't have three siblings. He could not know how competitive the oldest sibling can get. How sullen, envious, introverted, how desirous of peace and solitude. I was glad he didn't meet me as a teenager. He would have hated me.

I remembered Mama marching us all to get new winter outfits, and I would never know what to choose. Indecisive about colours and styles until someone else chose something, and then I would envy it. Suzanna was an easier child to please. She liked boots and scarves and shoulder bags resembling something out of a catalogue. Such flair. The problem was that unlike Suzanna – who was an embarrassing few years younger – I could not plump on a style. I had no notion of what suited me. I had a blue twinset chosen for me one winter, dark blue, to wear over a pleated tartan skirt. Mama insisted I wore her pearls. I was sixteen, and felt an ancient twenty-six.

Perhaps it was a mistake to reminisce and recall everything through my present anger. I could not shift the indignation, and could not talk to anyone about my present state of mind. Not even John. Especially not John, because he was the cause, root, and reason for it. Soaking, drenched in misery, I tried to sort everything out and make decisions about my entire life – what was left of it, at fifty-eight – trying to deal with the most enormous surprise that had ever shaken me out of myself.

And then Mama died.

Nigel's phone call came at a very bad moment. John in Queensland, all my siblings on the other side of the globe, my only old friend and confidante in hospital having a hysterectomy, and all in a heatwave so bad, so humid, so appalling I felt like rolling into a foetal ball and dying too.

When was the last time I felt happy? Impossible to remember. Now, here, in my old childhood bedroom, where everything rang dismal bells of memory, it was all coloured by a foul internal ferocity I could not shake off. If it weren't for the rage, I might have enjoyed being back. I squinted at the damp ceiling and thought about money.

Anyone else, in any sort of circumstances, would have been overjoyed to win so much money in such a flukish way. A single ticket, so serendipitously discovered, so stealthily redeemed, had the potential to change everything. But I had changed it all already. Or rather, John had. He would have said he changed things because I had changed. Did all marriages not go through phases like ours?

Not Mama's marriage – not hers, because Papa died too early to cause her rage. Outrage. Naked indignation, like John caused me.

He was so numb and fed up he packed and left for his Brisbane conference with infuriating slowness. The last thing he said, in the front garden with the taxi already there, was that he was not coming back. 'After the conference, Paola, I'm going onward ... look, I'm not coming back, okay? I'm not. I don't know a good way to say this, but ... I'll be staying in Queensland for a while.'

Astonished – was I astonished? – I could only repeat his words. 'For a while?'

'A long while. I've ... met someone.'

'Met someone!'

A straight silent mouth and wide eyes, surprised at his own words. Surprised to hear them repeated.

I was beside myself, but tried to hang on to dignity. It was not elegant or mature to get too ruffled, not with a taxi waiting, out in the front garden; but I could not help the words. 'You met someone. Teenagers say I met someone. Kids say *I met someone*. Adult men say, I had an affair and wrecked my marriage. That's what they should say, John.'

He got into the taxi, and waved, as if he waved to some acquaintance, some vague associate, and not his wife of twenty-eight years. He *waved*.

Bewilderment grew later when I discovered most of his things were packed in preparation, neatly, purposefully, into cartons in his study, a less sumptuous office than mine at the back of the house. Labelled carefully, all taped up, waiting to be collected, the cartons were more insulting than his last words. More puzzling than the last flutter of his hand, waving.

John was leaving me, and without much ado, without many words. There were no heated, defensive explanations.

Of course I understood why.

Crushed, insulted, I walked through the house. What I needed was a coffee. What I needed was a drink. Or a kilo of chocolate. With numb fingers I mixed myself one of my infrequent gin and tonics, with over-fizzy tonic water from a half-frozen bottle at the back of the fridge, lying on its side behind a forgotten bunch of celery.

It froze my throat, and bubbles went up my nose, but the gin warmed my empty stomach and I could breathe again. Slants of dreaded sun blazed through the garden windows onto the living room rug and I almost went to sit at my desk as I always did, but writing would not be possible. Not then. Not after being summarily left by my husband.

Off to seek his fortune, like Dick Whittington?

Fury bubbled inside me, and did not calm, even after Nigel's sad phone call, even after thirty minutes gazing blindly out at the hot white garden where I dared not go, with the phone still in my limp fist. We were all meeting in Fiesole for the funeral. How on earth was I to explain what had happened to me; to Nigel, Suzanna and Brod?

Two hours – which would ordinarily have been spent drafting a new novel, or rewriting another, or researching some important forensic or procedural detail for a future project – were passed in sore doldrums, pacing through rooms empty but for the accumulations of years spent together. There was one consolation: Mama would never know of my humiliation. My emptiness in this empty house. Full, but empty. Books; books everywhere. Souvenirs from many trips to Europe, several lavish presents and collections in which we could indulge, being childless.

It was one of the facets of our marriage that could have pushed John the way he went, the fact we had no children, and the fact it was because of me. How could I have said it was my fault if what did not conform to what he wanted was my physiology? How could I dredge up the sorrow of what happened to my first and only pregnancy? No one knew. No one but John.

He must have been angry too, and his emptiness and resentment spilled over his ability to stay loyal and committed. But now? After all those years? It was crazy.

I could have, must have, misread his contented resignation to a life full of travel, writing, cultural pursuits unhampered by years of nappies and bottles or the matters that burden other couples. What? School choices, inappropriate friends, expensive clothing? It was what Nigel and Harriet talked about when they were raising Lori and Tad. Blazers, musical instruments, dentists' bills.

It was obvious I misread his resignation, and how long it would last, because there he went – off to Brisbane, and never coming back. Whether or not there was anyone there waiting, to fulfil his family dreams, or smother him in sexual warmth for which I had no desire lately, was by the bye. I sought my eyes in the hall mirror and admitted, acknowledged, it was years since we had felt truly happy together.

John had hit the wall, and went off toward something better. My anger would subside with time. It was for me to make a more comfortable life for myself now. Perhaps it was time to take satisfaction in a future made up of solo decisions. Did I have a choice? I took a deep breath, more like a sigh, when I thought of not having to consult anyone when I wanted to do something or go somewhere.

Still, with shaking angry fingers, I texted John a brief message about Mama's funeral and my intention to fly immediately to Fiesole.

His response was equally terse. *Very sorry – condolences to everyone.* Terse. Terse.

There was a surprising brief spattering, though quite typical of Melbourne weather, of raindrops on the bedroom window when I dragged my suitcases out to pack for Fiesole. I watched the drops evaporate, from my perch at the end of the bed, still unmade from the morning, when we had risen and got out of bed, one on either side, together. Like we always did.

Always. Always. Always was over.

Bright as though the shower never happened, the sun swept and slanted in from over treetops beyond, and revealed the empty side, John's side, of the wardrobe.

All that was left were gently swinging naked wooden coat hangers, empty shoeboxes, three ties, and a brand new shirt with swing tickets still on it. A present from me he had never worn. Also, among the boxes and mothballs at the bottom, an unfamiliar piece of paper I had to inspect.

A lottery ticket – lotto. Something we never – or very rarely – bought. 'Lotteries are for people who are bad at maths,' John would say. So what was a lotto ticket doing at the bottom of his wardrobe? I stooped and picked it up, flattened it out from the way it had clearly been scrunched up, and scanned the lines of numbers.

Such hope in numbers, people placed, several times a week. I never believed in luck, and neither did John, I had thought. Yet here was evidence he had bought at least one, and disappointed with the outcome, had balled the offending thing and chucked it to the bottom of his wardrobe. An act of frustration I had never seen him commit, and yet, here it was.

It stayed on my dressing table for two days; physical proof of how we never truly get to know someone, even if we lie next to them each night, and rise with them in the morning. How we discover – sometimes too late – an aspect of a person we were too blind or too blasé to notice. So John did believe in luck; did believe he could change his life with money. When money didn't come to facilitate change, he ran off anyway. Such was the level of his disappointment with our life together.

I looked and looked at a framed photo of us, taken a short time into our marriage, all those years ago, searching his face and seeing it very nearly unchanged. Or so I thought. John was like Brod – a bit of grey in his hair, a couple of greys in his eyebrows, which was a source of jokes, a couple of lines on his forehead, and it was about all. Both boyish, both with smiles in their eyes, which hid true feelings. One had to wonder whether they were ever touched deeply by anything.

It was startling to note the similarities in my brother and husband, and how they were so real. Was it why I was attracted to John in the first place – that he had the same eternally youthful Peter Pan appearance?

Those young aspects were accompanied by behaviours equally juvenile; buying a lotto ticket and throwing it to the bottom of his wardrobe when his dreams did not come true. It showed me he had dreams outside our marriage, which I was surprised at because they did not match mine. Because they did not include me.

Humiliation and disappointment – some of the most affecting emotions in life – were conceivably what prompted me to gaze at the revealing ticket longer than I should have. Only to see the draw date was not months or weeks ago, but the previous day. The day Nigel said Mama died. When John was well on his way to Brisbane, to take his leave of a marriage without notice.

I tucked it into my handbag, and only remembered at the time of booking my flights to Florence it was there. Checking it at the newsagent's – even if only to make sure I had the date right – was only a reflexive thing. I went about my errands like an automaton, remembering to buy John his reflux medicine at the chemist's. Oh. Oh – I stopped just in time. He would have to get his own from now on. I pulled myself out of auto-pilot and had a quick coffee at a mall café I had never before sat at, determined to start changing things. The sad, miserable, futile determination of a woman on the far side of fifty.

The bells in the lotto machine rang out when I had the ticket checked, which told me two things. John had the draw date wrong, and the ticket was never scanned. The small Indian woman leaned forward from behind the counter and asked me to go in the shop. All her sentences were questions. 'I'm not allowed to shout it all over the shopping centre, you know – because of security? But you have won a large amount, ma'am? Which you will need to collect from the Lotteries people? I'll tell you what to do? It's quick and easy?' Her eyebrows rose, and her uneven lips smiled to show teeth on one side of a large mouth.

'No!'

'Yes – slightly over three million dollars? Congratulations?'

I had to hold onto the counter. I clutched my bag and stared at her, stunned wordless.

What followed were three days of dumbfounded movement. With the money safely clearing to my bank account, with my bags stowed somewhere in the bowels of an aeroplane, with my head crammed with innumerable emotions and questions, I arrived in Florence and made my way to Fiesole. In a rented car, a luxury at which I would usually have frowned.

My writing made me an adequate income, and John was by no means stingy, but having over three million dollars in the bank – in cash – was a very new sensation I would never get used to.

What went on in my head during the twenty-two hours it took to get from Melbourne to Fiesole was a repetitious debate with myself. Would I tell John about the win?

No – no. He did not deserve to be told. He had paid the fourteen dollars for the ticket, but leaving as he did, and leaving me in such misery, entitled him to nothing. I was so angry; so aggrieved. So wounded by his numb thoughtless exit from my life. Recompense in the form of a lot of money was my ... my what? My what? Just deserts. This one I could win. I was wronged, and the universe sent me compensation, instantly. All I wished was that John had said something dramatic like, 'I'm leaving! I'm taking what's mine! Damn you! You can have the rest!'

He hadn't, of course. John never spoke in forceful exclamations. He was measured, quiet, deliberate. His action that day, however, made me feel as though he had, for once, shouted his disgust at me.

The events of the last three days were overwhelming, incredible. If I had included them in a novel, readers would discount them as totally implausible. That so much should have happened to me, and all at one time, was not the stuff of fiction, however. It was all unaccountable in a way that could only happen in a life that was unfortunately all too real. All too overpowering. No one would believe me, but I was not about to tell a soul, least of all my siblings.

I saw Nigel and Harriet had some sort of struggle they would not talk about. The likelihood it was financial was quite high. I felt Brod did not care much about money. His career in banking brought in enough for him never to be worried. He lacked for nothing. Suzanna – the most prosperous of us four – oozed success like Mama's pancakes would ooze blackberry juice.

Ah – those pancakes. She had me in thrall, knocking a quiet knuckle on my door late on a Sunday morning, 'Paola – pancakes.' She made it special, so special – a change from Matilde's Italian meals and treats. At the kitchen table, just me and Mama. This was nothing like the biscotti or pasta the Italian woman whipped up so easily. It was nothing like the pistachio ice-cream, or delicious panna, the whipped cream the Italian maid floated on our bowls of milky coffee. It was nothing like dark crispy fried zucchini curls we clamoured for. Mama's pancakes were Mama's pancakes.

And now, having driven up the driveway, round the green cypresses, and parked near those slippery grey front steps, I had come close to making a decision about myself. Now I lay in the same bed I battled my adolescent demons in, I could think about what I would do – and how I wanted to live the rest of my life – so clearly it was starting to unsteady me. Or set me straight. Or something. I was never more confused in my life. Still, I had had a win.

I could spill the beans and tell everyone my marriage was over. It might either surprise them or not. I was not about to make it an announcement – I would tell them individually and in private. I would never tell a soul about the three million, however. It was impossible to know this early whether it would be enough to buy Nigel, Brod, and Suzanna out and take on the big house on my own.

Oh – as I turned a particularly sharp bend in the near-new rental car, I realized I had options, and it made me dizzy. Dizzy with the range and scope of what I could do with the rest of my life. Nearing sixty was not too terrible. Mama lived to well over eighty, and I could also have twenty good years left in me to take the place and renovate the guts out of it. Raise it to a reasonable condition, which would bring back something of the past. I wanted something of Mama's enthusiasm, her ability in the garden, her instinctual style, her understanding of exactly how a room should be decorated and furnished.

Was it what I wanted? I could not have known it as I climbed the front steps. When I took in the wall gods, when I leaned against the kitchen table, when I counted visible drops forming and falling from my old bedroom ceiling, I thought I could work it out.

Nigel

Dull and dreary

There was something decidedly strange about Brod. He'd changed in some way. He would never age, of course – he simply did not have the worries that accompanied having a family. Harriet and I have been through thick, thin, and all sorts of depths and widths of scrapes financially – and I had to admit, emotionally – since our two were born.

Lori was not an easy child. They say having an exceptionally intelligent and talented child is as much a problem as having a slow one, which we supposed was true, when she was very young. Tad was very much an introvert, and preferred messing about in his room, similar to what I liked to do in the kitchen when caught up in something insurmountable like too many bills in the same fortnight.

A child of the background, Tad was always, doing mediocre things effortlessly and without fuss.

Lori might have played the cello like an angel, but her brother blew a trumpet with quiet gusto in the school band and smiled his way around acquaintances and teachers in his vague mellow way. If he sniffed turbulence, he stayed away. We always wondered who he took after.

Come to think of it, there was something going on with Paola, as well. She was not as forthright and verbal as we remembered her. She found fault with the place, like a buyer ahead of an auction, enumerating negative aspects of the place, but more quietly. She watched us all, from the distance of the other side of the table, the entire time it took to have dinner the first night. I wondered how she would be the rest of the time; at the funeral, and when the will was read.

'The notary said he will come to the funeral, and afterwards we can all come back here from the reception – which should only take about an hour. He will say a few words and read the will.' I informed them all what had been arranged at breakfast on the second day. It was Harriet who organized it. I was not very good with timing things so they actually worked. From the expression in her eyes I could plainly see Paola would not have had the will read directly after the funeral. It could not be changed now.

My wife kept staring at my sisters. I thought she had decided for herself Brod would not make a fuss, and would agree the big house had to be sold, since anything else would be too complicated. It needed too much costly work to bring it to a state good enough to be rented out. Selling it was the only way.

I was still very uncomfortable about losing my job. The news would eventually filter out to everyone, I hoped, and I would not have to announce the information. At least – it was what I imagined would happen. I could always disappear to the kitchen to whip up a tiramisu or something. It was humiliating, to say the least.

'My goodness, Nigel! I've heard Matilde is still active and lucid and living in her own place.' It was Paola, who burst into the downstairs sitting room, wearing a bright shawl around her shoulders and holding a book.

I was surprised she did not know. 'Of course. We saw her a couple of years ago down in Prato, where she's living with a niece, I think. Deaf as a post.'

'Oh? How sad. She ... how old would she be?'

'Ninety ... no, ninety-two, I think.'

Paola sat in the old green sofa, grumbled about the dampness and the lack of lace curtains again, and went on. 'Do you think I should go down and see her? Do you think she'll be there tomorrow?'

I shook my head. 'Definitely too old for funerals, Paola.'

She leaned forward and dropped her voice a bit. 'Do you like Grant? He seems so staid and steady, and so much older than Brod.' She sat back and prepared to grill me.

'Not that much older. It's because Brod will never age. He's ... like a tall elf. Plus I feel Grant is very good for him – someone with an artistic bent ... you know, he designs buildings and does ... whatever architectural designers do.'

'Do you remember when he brought a flamboyant boy home for part of the holiday? Do you remember? Fletcher something, and how Mama cut him down to size ... and how we all ended up going down to put him on the train together?'

I shook my head.

'Don't you? It was hilarious. Mama understood Brod – always did, but his friend Fletcher was something else.'

'I don't remember, Paola.'

'He kept asking why two of us have Italian names and two of us have English names, and how we ate such different things from what he got at home.'

'Where was he from?'

'Somewhere in England – he was very bossy with Brod, and Mama soon put him in his place.'

I shook my head again. 'You were blessed with the memory of ...'

'It's a curse, not a blessing, Nigel. Some things I'd much rather forget.'

'Oh, come on now – we didn't have a bad time of it at all.' But I saw suddenly it was not our childhood she wanted to forget, but something that had happened to her, and it was most probably recent.

'You and ... is everything all right with you and John, Paola?'

She smiled and opened the book. Her downcast eyes did not tell me a thing. All I could see were the top of her head, with its severe haircut, and the upturned corners of her small mouth. Her lipstick was very much like Harriet's. A shade of dull apricot that went with her hazel eyes. Harriet had Lori to guide her – she knew more about cosmetics and what suited her than her mother. Paola – well, Paola was the kind of woman who would have loved a daughter.

'John's a bit overworked, Nigel. He couldn't even come to this.'

Was what I heard in her voice resentment? 'Oh.' Wouldn't it be nice if Paola could talk to someone? She was manifestly so full of grief over Mama. Harriet would not do. They never got on. Suzanna was too self-involved to fully listen. She asserted herself, always, and drew herself above and beyond us all. I wondered if being a twin did something to women.

'If it weren't raining, I would take a walk down to the rubble wall.'

'Part of it's come down, you know, Paola.'

'Oh no.' She paused. 'How much do you think it would take to fix this place, Nigel? Conservatively, I mean, if we ever wanted to ... do it up?'

'We?' I stopped. It was no time to ask if she would consider buying me out. It would have solved a lot of my financial problems to come into some cash. It wasn't the time.

'A rough figure.'

'Rough – not a lot. Something like ... what? A couple of ... okay. I did do some sums in my head about a year ago. 'Two hundred thousand euros, perhaps. Or three if you wanted to be lavish.'

'So much!'

I pulled a face. 'I know it sounds like a lot.' I

could not say more. Her face showed a mixed sentiment. She did not seem to like the figure. It was a lot of money none of us could pull together easily.

'Do you think Brod and Grant are interested in taking it on?' Her eyes were narrow. She must have thought of asking Brod to buy her out. I wondered how she would tackle the conversation. Paola could be quite imperious. It made me angry to think how calculating she was. It irked me that she did not consider me for a second. Was it so obvious I could not buy her out; did I appear that needy? But I had to control my temper. Mars, my wall god, my war god, was a childhood influence I could blame once upon a time. Not any longer.

'Oh, look. Is that a break in the weather? I think I will walk down to the wall.' She was off, leaving her book on the sofa, and the door ajar behind her.

I sat back and waited before putting the kettle on, wondering whether a whole kilo of veal medallions was enough for dinner. The thought of food calmed me, but I wondered whether I would be this much in control for the whole week.

Suzanna put her head in the door. 'There you are. What's everyone wearing tomorrow? Regulation black, all dull and dreary?'

'You would never be all dull and dreary, Suzanna. Ask Lori and Harriet. They seem to have it figured out. All I have to do is wear a dark suit. This is Italy, after all.'

'Hm. You boys have it easy. I brought this fabulous black outfit, but it definitely needs something to brighten it up. Like red shoes.'

I smiled. '*Red shoes* ... ask Lori and Harriet ... they'll tell you.'

It was time to start preparing dinner. There was a pile of beans needing topping and tailing, which was a nice contemplative task. The big blue colander could be in the great old scullery; I'd have to look.

Mama insisted on calling it a scullery, when of course it was nothing of the sort. It was an ancient annexe to the kitchen, presumably medieval, against which the whole house leaned. It felt like everything else was added to it. Sturdy and substantial, it must have started out as a stable, and was probably where all the livestock was kept when the weather was like this; too rainy for anything.

It had a vaulted roof, metal rings set at intervals along one side, and walls so thick the tall thin windows were like slashes in the masonry, through which light would slant if there were any decent sunshine outside.

It was getting dark, and Paola would have to find her way back by memory. I could imagine her lingering out there in the wet grass, under threatening skies. Brooding. She would brood. I would seethe. That's how we were.

The view through the scullery window facing down the back was limited, but I glimpsed her out there, walking, deep in thought. I was surprised when someone caught up with her. Someone in a big rainproof jacket with a hood. He brought along another jacket and helped her into it. I watched as they walked away from the house together, both grasping the hoods, bent against the wind and rain like old sailors. It might have been Brod, helping out our eldest sister, who was most likely feeling lonely, and not a little sad. John should have come out with her from Melbourne. He was usually considerate and quite sociable. Something must have happened.

Suzanna

Missing objects

The state of the house was nothing short of disastrous! I would have to get consensus from everyone ... the only rational way would be to sell it. On the market – right away! Of course it all depended on what was in the will, but it stood to reason we would get equal parts of everything. Mama would never have had it any other way.

I realized now how fortunate it was, from what I gathered after the death of a friend's father, and the complications she experienced, that Mama never remarried. Now she was gone, and from how everyone's expectation was building over the will, I wondered why she never did get married again. Was there never someone in the picture? We were so little when Papa died. Surely she would have met someone, or had some sort of relationship. It was strange I could not remember a single man with an interest in her. In any case – it was a good thing!

Romance didn't last, and brought complication.

My wall god, Apollo, peeling and mouldy, speckled with mildew, held nothing of his old enchantment. His bare torso was flat and flaking. Neither handsome nor magical, as he was when I was a child – when I dreamed he would float off the wall, land at my feet and kiss me – he badly needed painting over. How I wished I had a great can of grey paint and a wide brush!

I wandered all over the floors and the wing before and after dinner on the second day, while Lewis was walking Otto in long wet grass, which would have totally ruined my boots, and noted all sorts of things were missing. Paintings from the drawing room, several rugs on the ground floor, which were replaced, it seemed, by newer cheap ones, which had started to go funny – damp and rolling at the ends. What happened to all Papa's old things Mama had always insisted were not to be packed away? The ebony and ivory chess set, the old phonograph, the newer Philips record player, large and grey ... what else did I remember?

I would have to speak to Paola. She was the one with the elephantine memory! Was it possible Mama gave things away, or sold items without telling anyone? It was of course her stuff! She could dispose of anything and everything any way she wanted to. Some parts of the house seemed intentionally stripped, especially of paintings. I seemed to remember different items in certain places.

There was nothing I liked better than well-restored antiques against the sleek background of good architecture. Modern architecture, though, not this. We used to have pieces in the villa I could have happily taken away. Valuable pieces. Good English furniture! The perfect antiques. I wondered about it all.

Nigel and Harriet found it necessary to replace things like the kitchen taps when they were here caring for Mama – such practical things were obvious and essential; something I would have done too, and without delay! But other things were either neglected, like the outdoor furniture and the terrace awnings; or had completely disappeared, like the lace curtains and ... Goodness, where was the great big bookcase? The enormous antique bookcase in the passage to the wing had disappeared! I definitely had to ask Nigel about it.

'Suzanna, calm down.'

'I am calm! Haven't you noticed some things are gone?'

'Of course we have.'

How annoying he said *we* in that way, like he and Harriet knew everything about the house and its contents. They did know, of course, but it needed no verbal confirmation. I waited for him to continue, hoping he wouldn't say Mama had given it to them for their flat in London.

'She gave some things to Donato and Matilde. Some things were a bit beyond repair, so she had them taken away. I think other things might be back in Cornwall.'

'Oh! Could it be there, in that case? And the Cornwall house has been locked up ... vacant for a while, am I right? We'd better have it seen to, or it will fall into disrepair too!'

'I think there's a tenant in it right now. Oh, Suzanna. This place isn't so bad.'

I gave him one of my boardroom glares. I thought he deserved it. 'It would take several hundred thousand, Nigel – and you know it – to bring this place anywhere near acceptable. It's close to being uninhabitable. My bedroom ceiling drips!'

'It always has. Everyone's does ... a little.'

'Much worse than when we lived here.'

'We were always here in summer.'

'It needs a bucket! A bright orange plastic bucket in the dead centre of my floor!'

'Everything's worse for you.'

'Now don't you start! Of course I have standards. It's because of how we were raised. Mama ...'

'If it were the case, we'd all have the same standards.'

Well. He practically told me off for my tastes and criteria. Shabby was shabby. Broken was broken. Drips were drips. Surely Nigel could see how the Fiesole house had deteriorated. I let him go. I watched him wander off to his precious kitchen, where he always ran in times of stress ... and irritation. When we were young it was to get something to eat from Matilde. Now it was to drown his sorrows in cooking.

Things did not change much. Nigel was still Nigel.

And Paola was still Paola, it seemed. She mooched around checking everything and everyone, watching us in her typical silent way. Thoughts were plain on her face. I wondered she didn't know every thought of hers was broadcast on her forehead, in those dark little eyes and around her shrinking mouth. She ought to find a better hairdresser, was the first thing I thought when we arrived. Her too-short cut, that severe parting, and desperately needing professional colour. Lewis never noticed. He mumbled monosyllables when I told him on the first night; everyone seemed the worse for wear and age.

Paola was turning grey; skin, hair and even her eyes. Nigel was carrying the sorrows and problems of the entire world on his shoulders. A powder keg waiting to explode. Brod? Brod was smiling all over, but I could feel something was niggling on the inside. Besides, he now looked his age. His boyfriend was a far sight more attractive, and better groomed too. He should have taken a leaf out of Grant's book – and shop where he shopped for clothes. He was in banking, but those trousers, that sweater!

It was funny, because Brod always wanted what other people had. I'd have thought he would go for Grant's dress style. That man, gay or not, was well-dressed. Then again; those amazing features would look good in a hessian sack.

Pity about the big bookcase. It would have fitted perfectly in our hall. I would have liked to own it. As a matter of fact, I wanted it. Donato died years ago, but Matilde was still alive. She would be a hundred and six! Nigel said she was too old to come to the funeral tomorrow, but I would have to pay her a visit because she might know where the bookcase ended up. Prato, Harriet said. She lived in Prato. Lewis would have to drive us there and back. I would have to take along something in the way of a gift.

Now what would an old Italian woman appreciate? How would I know? Lewis would have to put on his thinking cap!

Brod

Rain, rain

'When the will is read tomorrow, Grant ...'

'I know, Brod. I know I'm not invited. I'm not family. Not yet, anyway. I have something else planned.' Grant's sincere expression was reassuring.

I watched him, filled with a bit of awkward uncertainty, but relieved his supreme tact and discretion would get us both to where it was more comfortable to be. Strange as it might have felt, I was getting used to trust, so late in life. I used to think I was trustful to a certain extent, but having three siblings, being a twin, hardly remembering my father, and being queer were not the ideal recipe. School dashed any feelings of confidence and buried any trust I might have had. Schools, especially boarding schools, should be abolished. They were horrible, cruel places and taught little of worth.

Anyway, it was years ago. Being with Grant was teaching me more than I could ever have got in high school, even though I had to admit I landed a perfectly good career in banking after university. I had to show everybody, didn't I? I had to show Mama and everyone else they were wrong about me being indecisive and weak.

There was something else on Grant's mind though, something other than how strange it was to lodge in town when there was such a big house to stay in. He insisted on going off on his own to explore Fiesole while the will was read. To explore Fiesole – how strange it sounded to me after all those years. It was home more than any other place, and I knew its lanes and steep winding streets better than anywhere. Better than Cornwall.

We drove up, to come to this house, Grant and I, flanked by those vertical masonry walls, rough hedges of unpruned laurel bushes and miles and miles of cypresses in ragged lines, and I could see he loved it on sight. He drove more slowly, and when we took a bend, gazed out over the valleys we rose above, gradually leaving Florence behind, leaving the densely-built parts, the narrow walled streets, the yellow-painted houses with green shutters, and ascended among the *poderi* – the vineyards and untidy olive groves. The greyness of grouped olive trees always meant home to me, but I only could name the feeling on the drive up. Strange. It was nostalgia. First time I noticed I was nostalgic.

The smell, too, the dank heavy wet rainy smell coming from the soaked fields surprised me with its wallop of memory. We were always there in the summer as children, and it was mostly dry and dusty, but we often got a good downpour before we went back to school in September, so we could distinguish the smell of doused citrus leaves, the olive scent, the laurel fragrance rising to our windows at the house, and the musty subtle but unmistakeable smell of drenched grapevines.

Even the purple hills in the distance, the terracotta tiled roofs of the farmhouses, and the straggly trees which seemed to lean over and hold the roadside banks from tumbling to the bitumen had their own special mental smell for me, depending on when we drove those roads.

'Turn your window down,' I said.

'What, in this rain?' But he did.

'See? That scent.'

'Ah, yes.'

An end-of-summer smell, or a beginning-of-autumn scent, which spelled the end of weeks of lounging around, reading. Wishing for a swimming pool; or wishing the house was somewhere closer to the sea.

Through Grant's eyes I could see we had a magical privileged childhood, the four of us. But time had passed. We no longer were Silent Paola, Angry Nigel, Greedy Suzanna and ... did they think I was still Hesitant Broderick? Indecisive? Dithering? Irresolute?

I wished some of us were less bitter, less inclined to remember the self-indulgent juvenile tendencies we had than the real people we evolved into in the end. The end ... well, it was the end for Mama. How cruel it was that I could not be here. Grant was right when he tried to reason with me, but there would always be the feeling I could have been present. I hoped the funeral itself would eventually give me some sort of closure. I realized I didn't definitely need to be at the New York conference, but I did go. How was I to know? Now, I needed closure. A cliché, if ever there was one.

'Brod, Brod – the bookcase is missing!' Suzanna was flustered. Impeccably turned out, but flustered. Her exclaimed words tumbled out.

'Oh – now I remember it. Yes. Ask Nigel ... but I know what he'll say. Riddled with woodworm and had to be burnt.'

She tossed a perfectly coiffed head.

Now I had a few grey hairs, she didn't, and I had great sticky-out ears, and so did she, but she appeared like she jumped straight out of a fashion ... no, a *business* magazine. She would not have seemed out of place up in the boardroom at my bank.

She tossed her head again. 'Incinerated? The beautiful Chippendale ... it had glass doors and everything!'

'What you remember best is getting on a chair and tracing the glass frames and mullions with your little fingers. Matilde would ask you to be careful not to fall, and not to get sticky fingerprints on the glass.' I could feel what was forming in her mind. She wanted it. She wanted the bookcase badly. Suzanna was like that.

Well, I could want it too. Not as badly as she did. I certainly wanted *something* from this house – to remember it by. What did I remember liking? All I could think of was tracing the design in the library rug, tracing the pattern as I lay on my stomach, listening to Mama read. I did it so long I still remember the border pattern. I was mad about those rugs, but it was too late. They had been replaced by others. Cheap synthetic ones without a nice pattern, which refused to lie flat.

Surely we could all find something nice to take away. Value was not an issue, although it would be nice to have something whose quality would endure. I saw my sister still stood there, waiting for an answer. 'Isn't that what you recall, Suzanna?'

'No it's not! I don't remember any such thing!'

I had to distract her. 'So Matilde would lure you into the kitchen for a biscuit with almonds in it.'

'A biscuit! I don't eat biscuits.'

I laughed. I had to laugh. 'You did in those days. Don't you remember what she called us? *Gemelli golosi.*' The memories came to me in sensations, in my head. I could smell the almond biscuits, feel the kitchen warmth, remember the way Matilde swept both fringes off our foreheads at once – a hand each, raking our hair back as if we were little ponies. 'Greedy twins, she called us.'

'I was never greedy, Brod.'

But she saw her inquiries about the bookcase were starting to give that impression. 'And the books ...' Her words petered out. She raised thin arms and dropped them limply by her sides, and started to turn away.

'The books would never have been thrown out. You know how Mama was. They'll be crammed in with all the others in the library.'

'Oh, yes.' She paused, hooked a dark wisp of hair behind an ear and quickly loosened it again; conscious of the impression she wanted to strike. 'Brod, it was a lovely, lovely piece of furniture. I wouldn't mind so much if Mama gave it away, but I'd hate to think it was burnt!'

'Do you remember hiding in the big bottom drawer?'

Her eyes flashed.

'Do you?'

'It was where Papa kept his collection of records. Now where do you think all those vinyl records went?'

'I hope they were given to Donato. Matter of fact, I think the collection did go to him a few years after Papa died ... or we'd never have been able to hide in there.'

She seemed to have a selective memory. With her mouth in a straight line, and a spine equally rigid, she tip-tapped on high heels towards the kitchen.

'What was that about?' Grant came up behind me. He knew, but didn't want to appear like he had eavesdropped on the entire conversation.

'Stuff. We remember different things.'

'You mean you remember the same things in different ways.'

I laughed. 'Or not at all.'

'Hm. Brod, come and look at the front.' His beautiful eyes were excited. 'The mishmash of architecture of this place is quite ...'

'Quite what? Mama adored it.'

'That's what I mean. It's a very happy conglomeration of additions ...'

'... and annexes and restorations and extensions, yes!'

'Over such a long time. How can you not want

to ever live here again?'

I punched him in the arm. 'Want or wish, Grant? You know it's impossible.'

'You said it yourself. You said you'd miss this place.'

'I ...'

He led me to the front and we stood under a leaden sky and a torn awning. I could see what he saw. The fanlights, balustrades, the terraces, the way the land fell away at the back to show such a splendid view past the terracotta roof of the wing, and the way the wing sprawled away from the ancient scullery, whose rough-mortared buttresses seemed to crumble before our eyes.

'And you did say your bank has a Florence branch, which would be happy to have you. You could work *down the road*.'

I started to see the germ of an idea in his eyes. 'Grant – please! It would mean buying the other three out. I could not possibly do it. The whole place would have to be gutted, restored ... practically rebuilt in places.'

'Money, money, money.' He pushed the sleeves of his sweater up to his elbows. 'Think of the fun, though.'

'Don't start rolling up your sleeves – you know it's financially impossible. Plus – what would you do in Fiesole? Think!'

But the glimmer in his eyes, and the way he squeezed my shoulder, told me it was not the end of the conversation.

'Anyone hungry?' Nigel shouting from the kitchen summoned us all from all parts of the rambling mansion.

'How much Italian do you speak, anyway?' I asked Grant as we drifted to the kitchen followed by Paola, who had a finger inside a clutched book, as usual.

'*Tantissimo molto.*' Grant's eyes danced with mirth as he uttered the mangled phrase.

We all laughed with him. I did not know what I would have done without him to break the hard layers of ice forming after the initial polite warmth that lubricated our first hours there. It wasn't only Suzanna's questions that stumped me.

In the dining room, eating Nigel's delicious saltimbocca, examining the labels – which seemed familiar – of two bottles of wine at either end of the long table, and waiting for the chatter to settle, I saw Paola and Harriet were barely speaking.

'Is your room all right, Auntie Paola?' Lori too had felt the chill, and seemed anxious to build bridges. 'Does the music disturb you?'

Sweet child. She didn't inherit pleasantness from her mother, who sulked and placed herself with some deliberation as far as she could sit from Paola.

My older sister smiled. Paola can be nice, I had to concede. She was nice and measured, knowing accurately and incisively how much sweetness to inject into a sentence when it was needed. 'What, your cello? Of course not, it's wonderful to have music in the villa. I'm glad you came up from the back house – it must be freezing down there. When Donato and Matilde lived here they had the great *sistema* going.' She examined each face. 'Does anyone remember?'

'*Il sistema riscaldamento*! Donato talked about it all the time.' Nigel grinned. 'He tinkered and tinkered with the central heating, even in the height of summer. I wonder how it went in winter.'

'It's going now.' His wife eyed him pointedly. 'We'd all be frozen to the core if it weren't.'

'Hmm – the radiator in my room is just warm to the touch.'

'And mine.'

'It was converted to electricity at some point.' Nigel poured wine. 'I can turn it up a notch if you like.'

'We never needed it in summer. We ran around in t-shirts, barefooted, for nearly three whole months.'

'And jumped on the train again in September, feeling scratchy, trussed and trapped in school clothes.' I pulled a face and everyone laughed again.

'Mama heaved a sigh of relief, I'm very sure, when everyone got on the train.' Harriet's voice was starchy.

'No, she didn't! She was nothing like that.' Paola's eyes were hard. 'She absolutely adored having us here all summer, and always said she wanted it to last at least another month. It was what she always said.'

Nigel's wife made a face. So – all Paola's memories; they irked Harriet. She resented her having such an accurate recollection of the family's past. Was it because Harriet was a sort of orphan? I would never know.

Harriet put down her fork. 'She was patient. With four of you here creating havoc, she must have had to be as patient as Job.' She meant it as a joke, and I laughed, but it was not a great success. The room fell silent.

I tried to steer us toward a neutral topic. 'Where did you get the wine, Nigel? You must let Grant and me get some wine. We'll ... we can drive into Florence, couldn't we, and ...'

'After the funeral, I guess. Yes – thank you. I mean ... no, Brod, no – there's no real need, I suppose.' Nigel pinched his nose. It was a nervous gesture of his I recognized. He took off his glasses and examined them for smudges. He seemed to be dreading the funeral the next day. We all were, but there was more. My baby brother seemed bothered about something.

It was very clear to me there was nothing wrong with his marriage. He exchanged smiles and gazes with Harriet, meaningful glances, which spoke of closeness. Grant had taught me how to watch couples in cafés, picking the ones whose relationships were intimate and sweet, those who had met recently, and those from whom contempt and resentment oozed visibly, simply from reading their body language. He called it watching the world go by, and it made us laugh.

I watched Nigel and Harriet, and from the number of times their eyes met at the table, it was clear they still got on famously, and could converse using silent subtle eye movements. There was something else bothering Nigel, which none of us might ever get to know. I hoped his health was fine.

I also watched Suzanna and Lewis, and surprisingly enough, they seemed fine too. Lewis was more than happy to take a backseat in my twin's life; seemed not to mind being a wallpaper husband, minding the dog, carrying her things. He seemed inordinately proud of her. He might have had more reason than any of us could guess. It could have been more than just about money. Or being an introvert. Or wanting her to himself. Who could tell?

'The wine, Brod?' Nigel spoke at last. 'It's from underneath the scullery. There's …' He seemed to have made a decision. Could he have considered keeping it all to himself? I doubt it. He was not the greedy sort. It was Suzanna and me who Matilde called greedy. *I gemelli golosi.*

I remembered. It came to mind quite naturally. 'The trapdoor and the little wooden steps!'

'*Su e giù, su e giù!*' We all sang together, the four siblings. It was automatic, the way Matilde had taught us to sing *Up and down, Up and down* when we took those wooden steps to the cellar.

Lewis, Harriet and Grant sat and watched us, with three completely different expressions on their faces.

'So there's still some wine down there, amazing!' Suzanna thawed out a bit and smiled.

'There's more than *some* wine.' Nigel rucked both eyebrows. I saw what it was – he *had* contemplated keeping it all to himself.

Paola attempted a smile too, after joining in the one loud verse we all sang at once. 'Lots? I do remember the racks Donato installed. They were diagonal boxes, sort of thing. Goodness – it must be nearly a half-century ago. Perfect for laying down bottles.'

'Yes, it must be some time,' I said. 'It is ages ago. I'm surprised there's any left to be had. I don't remember the racks going up. Lots, Nigel?'

He finished his veal. 'Hundreds of bottles, literally hundreds. I remember Mama buying part of the year's vintage from the fellow down near San Girolamo ... or was it near the Roman baths? In July, she would do it. And she bought some recently, before she became so frail, and Donato stacked the bottles. Not long before he died, and not long before she got ... unwell.'

Paola's turn to nod. 'Yes, and also from the old man up at the chapel, she used to buy wine. By the chapel, remember? He'd bring it down our hill in a van. Is it still all down there? No wonder it's so fabulous.' She sipped from her glass, and peered at the label on the bottle. '*Enoteca Bramduardi*. Aren't we lucky? This stuff is not bad.'

Talk drifted to plans for the following day, the order in which we would read, what everyone was wearing, and how we all would drive down to the church, and afterwards, onward to the cemetery.

'I still can't understand why it's all so ... why in a church?' I found it difficult to figure out.

Paola pursed her lips, like it was obvious.

'No, Paola – I don't understand.' Suzanna pushed a finger forward in front of her, wanting an explanation.

'She left instructions. Nigel said so – he told us. It's all written down. Time, place, music, readings ...'

Suzanna was still not content with the answer.

Paola went on, after casting around at each of us, in the way we were used to. 'Besides, we all remember Mama's fondness for ceremony. She delighted in ceremony, celebration – don't you remember our Christmases in Cornwall?'

'You mean ...'

'Yes – she meant it to be. She wants us all to go along to church tomorrow. And to sing.'

Paola

Curtains

Ceremony, in a little Fiesole church. Ceremony; a sea of unrelieved grey and black. Except for a blur of cut flowers. Aside from their scent held inside the dome, the combination of churchy scents; stone, dust, incense. Must and mould; grey and black, black, black. Except for Suzanna's red shoes.

If she'd asked me, I suppose I'd have said she could wear what she liked. My young sister always did what she liked. That was the difference between us: I always felt I had to do the right thing and fade into the surroundings, like some silent camouflaged moth, and she burst into rooms expecting everyone to be waiting with bated breath for what she was yearning to tell. The brilliant imago.

After Papa died, everyone changed a little. Nigel wanted to take over and 'do things for Mama', Suzanna grew more noisy and demanding, and Brod gardened, getting mud on his shoes and dust in his eyes. I retreated into my books and music, carrying my heavy transistor radio around on its leather strap. The batteries were expensive.

'What is it, Paola?' Mama was patient with me. Should I ask? 'My ...'

'Your radio? Batteries? You can ask for batteries, darling. Come here. It's not a problem. Donato will bring you batteries when he goes down to Florence for things.'

And he did.

But Suzanna would burst into the kitchen, already talking, talking, talking. Demanding a new bathing suit and sunglasses, like she saw in a magazine, without waiting to think, without pausing. Mama would smile and promise to get her some things too.

'But I'll have to wait all summer!' Her young plaintive voice. Always pulsing through the house.

Mama put down whatever she was holding, beamed with love and patience, and explained that a few days was not all summer.

One of those hot and sultry summers, for some feast day which took place in Florence, we were all given confectionary. The boys had sticky boiled sweets packed into wooden pencil boxes. Suzanna and I received chocolates in little cases, which converted into jewellery boxes when everything was eaten and the wrappings were taken out. I wanted the blue one, but Suzanna got it, and I had to be content to take the red one. I treasured it, for some reason, and kept my bead bracelets and funny little necklace charms in it. I kept it. I remembered packing it away to take to Australia after I met John,

85

almost twenty years later. I would have to ask Suzanna what happened to her perfect little blue box.

The church pews were hard and cold, the scent of flowers a stain on the memory – one I knew would not be erased in a hurry. I could not smell cut flowers again without thinking of this sparsely peopled yellow-walled church with its over-elaborate crucifix and damp guttering candles.

The coffin on its ornate trestle was an emotional cross we all bore in silence. A horrible silence broken by music over a bad sound system someone should have tried to moderate to our purposes. Too loud, too tinny, it would spoil the way I thought about those orchestral pieces forever. I suppose Nigel had enough to organize, and could not attend to every single detail.

I winced as I waited for the end of the Pärt recording. The church bells over our heads rang while it was playing, which robbed the bell in the orchestration of its mournful effect. Something, I had to concede, which was on balance not the end of the world.

I heard a hissed whisper to my left. It was Suzanna. 'I can't believe you left Papa off the card, Nigel!'

He peered at her blankly. I could feel him thinking, *It's Mama's funeral.* He'd be blaming himself for something he didn't do, because I searched inside the card, scanned the lines of small print, and yes, there it was; *Widow and loving companion of Roland Larkin.*

I felt like turning to hush my sister, and tell her

to read the card properly, but it would have been too rude. I sat still and steady, filling my mind consciously with stuff of the past.

Radio batteries coursed through my head before the readings began, and jewellery boxes, and shoes caked with garden soil, and missing gloves, and curtains, and a painting. A very special painting. Curtains again.

Curtains. I swallowed back a lump in my throat when I remembered what happened earlier that day. I stumbled in on Brod, an hour before we all started for the church, standing in Mama's sitting room. He was sobbing into a bunched-up handful of curtain.

I stopped where I stood and wondered whether I should slowly and as silently as possible back out again, but he looked up. 'So damn ... so abominably sad, Paola.'

I felt for him, and was choked up myself. What a terrible thing this was. How cruelly it brought back all that was wonderful about Mama. What we had lost. How it showed us all up for what we essentially were. Sentimental Broderick, hard-as-nails Suzanna, belligerent Nigel, and ... what did they think I was? Silent? Contemplative?

Nigel

Suppressed anger

A funeral is not the occasion to have an explosive tantrum, but it was undeniably what I felt like doing. I could have howled to the vaulted stone roof of the yellow church in annoyance. So I avoided Paola's eyes. I averted my face from Harriet's questioning glances. I dodged Brod's clearly mystified gaze, and cast my eyes away from Suzanna's direct stares. They all knew I was upset at the way the flowers had been placed, the positioning of the trestle, which I had asked specifically to be placed to one side, and which stood directly in the centre, in front of the altar. I recoiled when I heard the crude recorded music, which emerged from an ancient system in a harsh metallic high-pitched whine; and at how everyone placed themselves completely out of the order I had described the previous night. Did they do it on purpose? Annoying Nigel was becoming a family sport, exactly as it was when we were children.

Paola was especially exasperating. All she wanted to do was talk about the inheritance, and I had to stop her the previous evening. Talking about money at the table was not something we did. Mama was always elegant and circumspect about such matters. It was crass, materialistic, and vulgar, and Paola knew it. She insisted on saying, on repeating, that we all needed to discuss what might happen after the will was read.

Well – how could we discuss anything before we knew what Mama intended? It was highly likely she would leave everything to be neatly divided into four. The fairest and most equitable way to go. Harriet and I knew we deserved more than a quarter, but who were we to argue with Mama's wishes, if that's what they were? Who were we to enter everyone into a contestation against their will?

'But what about inheritance tax?'

I glared at her and her small bobbing head, afraid to open my mouth. I might blurt out something to regret later.

'What about it?' Suzanna never failed to respond when the subject was money.

I began to despair of my siblings. They were not what they were when we were young. They were worse. Suzanna more materialistic, Brod more lackadaisical and uncertain, and Paola ... ah, Paola! She defied description and comprehension. Fastidious and fussy, she looked down her nose at me and Harriet, making us feel we did everything wrong and organized everything badly. I did not even bother to stop and think what they all thought I was capable of.

Coming close to growling at Paola, I spotted Harriet's gaze – a plea to contain myself – and retired to the kitchen, where I fiddled with dessert and opened another two bottles of wine. Alcohol might mellow them, even though they were all beyond hope. Why did Lewis not get Suzanna to be a bit more sensible? Why did Grant not influence Brod – who could have done with a bit more sense? And Paola, all alone, without John to nudge her into a more positive outlook, put a damper on the entire event. I would be glad when the week was over and Harriet and I were back in England to attend to our sorry financial situation. It was becoming more urgent by the day. What I was to inherit – no matter its value – was to be without a doubt a quarter share of fuss and bother. The sooner divided and finished, the better it would be.

I would be the first one to sign the acceptance, to show the way. The sooner we all got out of any dealings with each other the better. I would have to keep a tight lid on my volatile mood for as long as possible.

But it was not to be. We emerged from the church and all made our way to the cars. Mama was to be interred at the *Cimitero degli Inglesi*, down the hill in Florence.

'I don't know why it wasn't arranged for her to be buried at the villa.' Paola was heard by all, even though I felt she tried to keep her voice low.

I moved to face her.

'Nige!'

I ignored Harriet.

'Dad!'

I turned away from Lori, who extended a hand to hold me back. She grimaced hopelessly at her mother.

'Paola – Mama left her wishes on paper. She wished to be buried at the English cemetery. She wrote it down! She arranged it. All I did was manage it. Time it. Book it. But it was she who wished it to be done so!'

She looked at me strangely, but said nothing.

'I wish you'd stop criticizing everything I do.'

'I don't.' She seemed as prissy as a sixteen year-old. The sixteen year-old who watched primly from the upstairs terrace balustrade when we three clowned around on the grassed terrace. The same one who refused to join us when we cycled down to the shop for ice cream.

My voice rose, filling the church forecourt, making even passers-by look round to see what could be causing such a fuss at a funeral. 'Find something nice to say, for once in your life.' I regretted the words the instant they were out of my mouth.

'I'm going to forget you said that, Nigel,' she whispered. Her smile was neither condescending nor humorous. What was it? What was she thinking? I stood there until Harriet tugged me into the car by my sleeve.

And she did. Paola did seem as if she'd forgotten, and was cordial and impassive at the cemetery, where I wondered what strings Mama had pulled with the Swiss church that ran the place, to get herself buried in that historic place. I would have liked to be there on a less emotional day, to read the place like a history book, to try to make out all the inscriptions in so many languages.

It would have been peaceful and healing to gaze up into the faces of those mortified stone skeletons, those angels racked by loss and remembrance, and recover alone. The stone they were carved out of was a paradox. Everything crumbled, but some things were eternal, like guilt. I had put my family in an untenable financial bind, and I wished I was there alone, or alone with Harriet.

As it was, I quickly became overcome by the sadness of the reason I was there. For a moment, I felt totally alone. Everyone evaporated, a silence fell about me, and I was rid of all my money problems, all my siblings' dilemmas, all my children's expenses. Alone in a bubble – a silent space, where no one existed apart from me and Mama, who was going away forever.

I didn't feel foolish when I waved at the coffin, which was lowered faster than I anticipated into the dark hollow. The rain started again as we all got into the cars and made our way upward from Florence. I could not wait for the dreaded reception to be over, so we could ascend back all the way along Via San Domenico, to the villa.

Brod

Singing in church

Grant looked splendid in his dark suit and gunmetal grey shirt and tie. They all stared at him, disbelief plain on their faces that he was there with me, my partner. How could Brod possibly land someone so statuesque, so handsome, they must have thought. What's more, in my fifties – incredible. It was about time they thought I did something great. Something only I could do. Mind you, it was still surprising to me, and I sometimes pinched myself that someone so calm and successful and good-looking was interested in me.

He was supremely tactful and kept to one side, both in the church and at the cemetery. The long drive between the two places was quiet. Too long, too bright, with the watery afternoon sun in my eyes as I drove. We had Tad with us in the car. He sat at the back and didn't say a word. Still in his tight school blazer, he wore a thin black tie as a concession to the occasion. I saw in the rear view mirror he hung his head often, lolling forward as if dozing off, and starting up again when his head nodded. It could have been the warmth and motion of the car, an endearing thing.

He didn't say a word, but I had heard him singing in church; a surprising clear, high tenor voice in perfect time, even with canned music coming forth from poor quality speakers at an embarrassing and startling volume.

Nigel's face was a picture of horror. He could not have foretold or avoided the atrocious acoustics, but he flapped his arms, frustrated, pushed to some sort of reaction, and I could see Harriet was hoping he would not erupt during the proceedings.

Luckily, everything went rather well if one omitted my reading, but I expected to be wound up and emotional. I did my best, but could tell from the way Grant sat he was waiting, waiting, for the whole thing to be over.

Mind you, I was dreading the reading of the will, because I knew Nigel would resent someone like me, with no children, no debts, nothing like the enormous responsibilities he had, would receive an equal quarter of Mama's estate, same as his. I doubted there would be any surprises. There was the house in Cornwall, the villa up in Fiesole, and all the bits and pieces accumulated during her lifetime. I knew there was some source of private income, whose type and value I was unaware of, but no one discussed it.

Paola wanted to, at dinner the previous night. Nigel's face prevented any discussion of the kind.

Suzanna and Lewis talked about their boating plans, which was foremost on both their minds. It sounded like a pretty solid plan, and I imagined whatever they inherited would simply make their boat-buying exercise a bit easier.

I was starting to regret having to sell the villa, and stood at the big back window before we went in for the reading, and gazed out towards the back. It was darkening to pitch black from indigo, with a few twinkling lights in the distance. Left to myself, I used the calculator on my phone to make a few quick estimates of what it would entail to buy my three siblings out. I bit my lip, and imagined Mama in the armchair behind me, bidding me wait. All the calculations in the world couldn't figure something that, until the reading, was a closed box. It was purely hypothetical, a silly conjecture, and wouldn't tell me a thing.

I pocketed my phone.

'I think the funeral went well, Brod.' Grant came up behind me. He had changed into jeans and sweater, and handed me one of two wine glasses he held.

'Adequately well. Nigel nearly lost it before we all got into the cars.'

'Everyone was wound up. Your older sister was in tears. Suzanna's husband got a bit teary too.'

'Lewis?'

'Hmm. How well did he know your mother?'

'Well enough. Mama knew us all very well. I think she liked him quite a lot, and thought he was a very appropriate partner for Suzanna.' This was enough to trigger a memory I had of my twin and her

95

string of weird teenage boyfriends. She adopted their habits, dress, activities, and accents while she was 'in love', which either dismayed Mama, sent her into silent shivers of laughter, or made her roll her eyes. 'I think Lewis was a surprise to us all. Mama did not think it would last.'

'And look at them.' Grant seemed to think they had a good relationship.

'Hmm. Look at them.'

'Suzanna hasn't stopped talking about the wall gods. She wants them painted over.'

Grant's eyes widened. 'The frescoes in the hall? You're joking. They're magnificent.'

'She says they're a mess and the whole space would improve if painted pearl grey.'

'No! No – whoever ends up with this house ... and I wish it could be us, Brod, I do wish ...'

I smiled. 'I know you and your wishes, Grant.'

He elbowed my arm. 'They usually come true. Whoever gets this house should have the frescoes restored. Properly, by someone talented and patient.'

'And cheap.'

'Hah! Not necessarily. Think of all those back bedrooms. That large space downstairs would make a perfect meeting or conference room ... or indoor reception space. There should be a pool at the spot you showed me ... and the grassed area above the terrace is perfect for a marquee.'

'Grant!'

'No – true. Think about it.'

I raked my hair back, seeing he had spent time thinking, considering, and undoubtedly calculating what it would all cost. 'What – weddings, parties, anything? Grant, all four of us, and our various spouses and children, would never agree about Thing One.'

He shrugged. 'So I see. You and Suzanna ... never, although she's your twin. Two more different characters I have never met. You and Nigel ... warfare. He's only just in control, and quite volatile. Not malicious at all, but not totally organized. I doubt he has any financial nous. You and Paola ...'

'Yes?'

We both swivelled to Paola's voice in the passage.

'Thought I'd find you two down here. Did I hear my name?'

I spoke quickly. 'Have you ... we were wondering about the reading. Is the notary ready to start?'

'We're *all* wondering about the reading of the will.' Her mouth was a small straight line. 'There aren't many alternatives or options. We're going to be left the awful task of selling everything, paying the inheritance tax, and dividing the spoils. I wish we didn't have to. I've wondered and wondered ...' Her eyes held something I hadn't seen before. A glint of something. 'The task should not be left to Nigel, whatever we do – he's done enough organizing.'

'They did a marvellous job of looking after Mama.'

Her head swung from side to side in half-agreement. 'Something tells me the will might recompense Nigel and Harriet in some way.'

'But how?'

'They're all in there waiting. The notary is

about to start. Let's go in.' She smiled at Grant.

It made me quite happy to see Paola and Grant get on so well. There was something compatible between them, my partner and my older sister. She was visibly more relaxed in his company, and it was obvious Grant wanted to know and like my family.

Suzanna

The people behind events

The notary, Dottor Umberto Ugobaldi, shuffling papers and peering up at us four in turn, over those dated metal-rimmed glasses, was like something out of a clichéd movie of the eighties. Truly as bombastic and pretentious as his splendid name. When he stared into my eyes I imagined – what a peculiar sensation – I had been especially favoured in the will he was about to read. The thin smile, the subtle rise of his prominent chin.

Then I saw he gave Paola the same gaze, when she entered, unusually late, with Brod. Grant had wandered off on his own. The notary scanned the room, only to pull back and look directly into Nigel's face, with a tacit meaningful smile. When his narrow-eyed scrutiny swung round to Brod, there was the ingratiating expression again. By the third time, I saw it was absolutely meaningless, and that he smiled in such an absurd quasi-meaningful way at

99

all his clients, whether they were listening to a will being read, a parcel of land being sold off, or a contract about some factory or other. If he handled the sale of one of my franchises, he would undoubtedly put the advantageous smile to good use.

There was no need for him to offer condolences, or to launch into a speech, because he had earlier spoken to us outside the cemetery. With the startling statuary behind him, the constant hum of traffic circling the oval burial ground, the lichen on drystone walls, which solidly retained the central mound, and the damp cypresses behind him, he mumbled his words of sympathy, in Italian, with narrow eyes behind glasses sparkling in the watery sunshine. '*Ecco*,' he said, to finish off, and we all thanked him at once.

For some reason of Mama's I shall never fathom, we hosted a quick intimate reception at a church hall not far away, where three nuns in short habits and abbreviated grey wimples inclined their grey heads and smiled at us. There were – of all things – small English sandwiches and tea, which the Italian guests regarded with curiosity.

'Who did the catering, Nigel?' I had to ask.

He mumbled something unintelligible and moved away to talk to someone else. Finally, we all climbed into the cars again and drove up to the villa. I hoped Dottor Ugobaldi would give us enough time for me to get out of the red shoes, which were killing me. The heels had sunk into the damp grass at the cemetery, and I hoped they were not ruined.

From the passenger window of our car, Lewis

and I could see Nigel, animated, talking to Harriet in a way I recognized as his angry mood. It was obvious Nigel had come to the end of his rope, and was allowing anger to drive him every which way! It was funny in certain respects. He hadn't changed. Tempestuous Nigel, whose fiercest emotion was fury.

Brod had changed only a bit, since it was easy to see being with Grant had calmed him considerably, but it still took him ages to decide about anything. The agony and long-windedness of what would happen when it came to the division of the inheritance was going to prove painful because of Brod. He dithered and ducked and wove every time there was an alternative, a fork in his path! Dealing with Italian bureaucracy was enough in my opinion. Adding Brod to the mix would be pure murder!

What could I say about my big sister? Still tongue-tied and woefully introverted, the transparency of her thoughts was as observable as her stubbornness. Insistent in a silent way. She disapproved of everything with scarcely a word. On this occasion, though, I felt there was something pulling and pushing at her. Did she think we were all Mama's favourites apart from her, and calculated she'd come out the worst in the will? Goodness knew. So calculating, was Paola, I sometimes wondered if she ever glimpsed the people behind the events, behind the figures.

Something was biting her, and she was not about to tell. Not to me, at least. Definitely not to Harriet. My sister Paola was not the confiding sort, and always felt better with complete strangers, which is why I thought she liked Grant better than any of us.

She had stood next to him at the reception, rather than talk to the nuns. Now, she sat quietly, nodding occasionally, listening to the notary's long-winded legal spiel. Such an eager face! Such straight thin lips! Our old maid Matilde used to call Brod and me the greedy twins, but the greediest of us by far was Paola.

Paola

A forgotten photograph

I was surprised, but certainly not disappointed, by Mama's will. The notary's English was good, and I was grateful Mama chose him so well. After his initial long-winded introduction in Italian, he lapsed into formal English, so there were no language hurdles to vault. Still, the complication of what he read us was impossible to unravel; and it was plain after the time he spent explaining the complexity of Italian succession law. He said there were two kinds of succession, intestate and 'testamentary' succession.

'You are all four of you very fortunate to have had such an intelligent and far-sighted mother. She has left a very detailed testament, which means a lot of time will be saved, because of the clarity and the fairness she achieved by understanding the law.'

Still, surprises filled the day. I excused myself and left the room when he was finished, making for the far field behind the house in the dark, until I walked into the railing overlooking the lane leading down to the street. It was covered with creepers and weeds. Light from street lamps below helped my eyes adjust to something more than darkness.

Revelations were the order of the day. First it was Suzanna turning up in a designer batwing outfit in deepest black, accessorized with brilliant red shoes. Mama would have loved her for it, even if it was less defiance or thumbing her nose at Italian convention than a stand for attention, but all eyes went to Suzanna's feet. Why I kept thinking of those red shoes was not clear. It was more envy than annoyance. She carried it off.

It was the second time I saw my nephew Tad during the weekend. I did hear his voice, though. He stood at the back of the church in a too-small threadbare school blazer, combing a nervous hand through his hair several times during the service. He disappeared soon afterwards and was absent at the reception, where we all were served tea and delicate English sandwiches, which some Italian guests regarded a bit curiously. Suzanna observed there might be a few Italian funerals adopting the strange catering after today. It was all about trends, she said. She should know, being such an entrepreneuse.

My reading, and hers, went well. I read first, and when I listened to Suzanna, felt disappointed in my voice, my lack of elegance, and the altogether awkward figure I presented. It was partly to do with my mood, I suppose, my preoccupation with John, and the fear grief would overwhelm me in the middle of a sentence.

Well, whether he ever existed or not, whether I believed in him or not, it was not my wall god

Neptune, but Saint Paul, who was by my side as I read his letter to the Thessalonians, and I did not miss a word or mumble, or have to take a sentence from the beginning. It was when I stopped wondering why Mama had chosen the reading. It was the bit about church traditions, and without a doubt the mention of work ethics. Traditions, traditions – she held them, broke them, respected them, felt they were like anchors in her life.

I was quite cool in the end, and looked up to see a blur of faces in front of me. The group was intimate, with only a few people there. I was surprised to see our old neighbours from Cornwall, the Edisons, who talked a great deal to Nigel and Harriet outside afterwards. Nigel said later they were staying in Florence and might pop up to the house in a day or two.

To my utter surprise, Nigel read a long piece from one of my books, which he translated himself into Italian. It was not a great success in my opinion, but seemed well received, and I felt it satisfied him in some weird way, which was, I supposed, the main use for funerals apart from celebrating the life of the departed, and furnishing some sort of elegant, human conclusion to a life.

Brod surprised me by faltering during his reading. He had to swallow hard and found it difficult to go on. The silence in the space when he paused was not embarrassing, but endearing. He surveyed the scene and seemed to take in the lilies, the candles, and everything he found – because we were all so unused to churches – a bit startling and awkward. I think he too felt the sympathy awash in the church for him. His high voice was a touch too loud, but much more contained and more muted when he continued, and I felt for Grant, in the row of seats behind me, who felt as though he held his breath the entire time Brod was reading.

Why Harriet wore such a drab coat and a French beret was beyond me. It was as if she went out of her way to make herself dull and dreary, in Suzanna's words. She didn't wear her usual lipstick, either, and went for a shade that blurred the outline of her lips to a wine-coloured smudge.

It was a grey day and we all wore grey and black. If not for the splash of Suzanna's red shoes, it was bleak and cold and grey, grey, grey; until Lori played her cello, which gave the proceedings a bit of a lift. Harriet had passed around cards printed with the order of readings and music, and I did read *Ombra mai fu*, but no one said it would be played by Lori. Beautifully done, I did concede, and very appropriate. A difficult piece to play unaccompanied, but she is a talented girl. Handel is always fitting, in a way.

I closed the card – stiff, and the colour of clotted cream – and folded it, and was startled to find on the front an oval portrait of Mama in black and white, which Nigel must have found in some old album. *In remembrance of Nina Larkin*. It appeared to have been taken when Papa was still alive, and showed her young and healthy, with eyes almost squeezed shut and untidy hair which meant she was out in her beloved garden. Not one I would have chosen if he'd asked, but I supposed it was quite a suitable choice in the end. I stared and stared at it, and remembered the way she would stamp her feet on those mats before tracking soil onto the tiles in the lower room overlooking the hills at the back. How she would laugh at her own badly-pronounced Italian. How she would gather us together in the kitchen and dole out little errands and tasks, which had to be completed before we could all sit down to some board game or other, or before she would drive us all to the communal swimming pool at Sesto Fiorentino.

My shoes hurt, and I wished I had worn something warmer. I wished for thick socks. I wished for a companion I could exchange glances with. Someone to hold my hand. There was no one in the world who could take the role. Unaccompanied, I felt like a maiden aunt, a spinster, despite having emerged – quite in one piece, I suppose – from a long marriage. I was uncomfortable and longed to return home. For the first time in my life ... no, it could not have been the first time; I yearned for a daughter. She would have led me home. I swallowed hard.

Where was home? I was suddenly drifting and had no anchor, no home port. No real mooring. If my home in Melbourne had any meaning left, it was the location from where John had left. Had left me. I was starting to form the unfortunate decision to sell, despite all the thought and love I had poured into the place. Ah – the gorgeous garden, the absolutely perfect rooms. They would now serve only to mock what it was all about. Comfort without warmth, with no sympathy, would be the only thing they would provide.

Did I only think such thoughts because I was so

far away? I needed a home rather badly now, and my old room up in the Fiesole house would have to serve. Nigel would have to 'turn up the heating a notch', however, or I would die of cold and damp.

One of the final clauses in the will left us all perplexed. We were all urged to pay special visits to Matilde, on separate days, in order not to tire her out. Why Mama made it so plain in the will was understandable to a point, but mystifying in another way, since it was inevitable we would visit the old woman who was such a faithful old nurse, cook, maid, nanny and everything else to us in our childhood, for the last time. She and Mama had a special friendship and understanding. Of course we would all go. She did not have to bid us to do so in such a formal, legal way. The notary peered over his glasses at us, one by one, giving Brod's name three firm syllables, *Brod-er-rick*, and nodding when he saw agreement in all our eyes.

What he might not have been prepared for was our gasp when the details of who was to get what were read. I was left stunned, stunned, but rather satisfied. I had never expected such an outcome, and of course deciding whether it was equitable was not an issue, because it was clear Mama had calculated the values of properties very, very carefully. Recently, too. We all gave each other silent stares when the notary read the date of the will. It was barely five months before she died. He explained how he had made his way to the hospice and ascertained and confirmed she was of sound mind and good intent – as signified by two signatures of competent witnesses, one of them Mama's doctor – to dictate a will to nullify and cancel all others.

'The aspects of Italian law were all followed to the letter – of that she made absolutely sure.' He lowered his eyes to the papers, and up again. 'And of course I was there to guide her in each of the aspects.'

I did not have a sense, when we all emerged from the library where we had all gathered, how any of the others might feel about the contents of the will. There were a few details about some small items. I was to get all the books in the house, and Papa's youthful portrait by Daniele Brigante. Nigel was given the entire collection of marble busts and some of the wine; Suzanna all the clocks and barometers of the house, which amounted to quite a number, and some named pieces of furniture she might choose from an inventory; and I was happy to hear the chess set, three paintings, and various bits and pieces of Papa's, which were in safe dry storage, plus more than half of the wine store, were to go to Brod.

Each single piece of her jewellery was itemized, valued, and apportioned to one or the others of us, and it was touching to listen to it detailed, and equally poignant to see how fairly she had figured it all out. Among other things, the pearls I hated went to Nigel for Harriet and later for Lori. The emerald earrings went to Suzanna, whose eyes brightened at once. Brod was given the beautiful gold Swiss wristwatch Papa used to wear when we were little, and I ... I was happy to hear her brilliant set of diamond rings was mine.

Lori came in at the end with a tray on which

Harriet had prepared a bottle of grappa and a host of small stemmed glasses. Dottor Ugobaldi stood and joined us, and elegant discretion demanded we did not discuss the will at that point. Discussion about the other astounding bequests would have to wait until he got into his lavish Alfa Romeo and whizzed down the driveway, past the cypresses in a row, past the dismal and ugly empty pots, which should have been full of some sort of shrub, and down the winding hill towards Fiesole and his home or office. That was an opportunity for me to disappear.

'Where are you going Paola? Aren't you ...?'

I swept past Nigel. He was beaming, so pleased about Mama's foresight and benevolence he was dying to talk about it, to gauge our agreement – or resentment – about his very good fortune.

I was not about to discuss Mama's wishes with him. Not right at that point. I could not help one observation. 'You did play a requiem in the end, Nigel.'

Surprise paled his face. 'Er ... um ... Mozart's. Only recorded music – did it sound okay? The sound system was appalling. I know Mama did not put it on her list, but ...'

'But?'

He seemed close to rage. 'Listen, Paola. Trying to please everyone is darned difficult. We had time for one more piece, so I thought, what would be appropriate? And we all did sing rather pleasantly to *Abide with me*.'

I held back a sigh. 'I'm not scolding, Nigel. Only making an observation.'

He took a deep breath and hurried into his

question. 'So what do you think ...?'

'Not ready to talk about it yet, Nigel. I don't want to talk about money and houses and ... or anything of the sort.' And I took off across the front veranda, past the drenched marble table. Someone, possibly Harriet, had taken away the fallen beach umbrella, and wound back the awnings over the French windows, so it was tidier out there than when I had driven up the first day. All in honour of the notary, who would not have given a second glance to such things.

I was not ready to discuss my own fortune with my little brother. Or his. No way. No. Not yet. I could scarcely believe it myself. Clever Mama. Clever, clever Mama. She knew us all so well, even in her old age, after we had all flown off to live out our individual independent lives. To live out our problems.

I walked down to the grass terrace where the large pots stood, stopped, and gave them a visual test. All still sound and usable. Huge and round-bellied, they stood, sodden and darkened by the rain, only half full of spent soil, with dead sticks which were once shrubs, blackened with mould, sticking out, all angled in defeat. I pulled one out and it came away without protest, so I threw it to one side and saw when I peered in the gloom there were dozens of tiny little green shoots, less than a centimetre high, pushing their way through the cracked surface.

New life. New plants. New weeds. There was a chance someone might see to them soon.

Nigel

Up and down, down and up

How sad to see Brod stop during his reading, close to tears. He swallowed and continued after a pause which was not too long, but he must have felt awkward. I sympathized, and gulped at the same lump in my own throat. He could not have remembered Papa's funeral. We were all so young. I can't remember what happened very clearly. Did we stay on at school? Hardly.

But here, now, in Fiesole, it was different and strange because no matter whether we had been to other funerals, I did believe none could ever be like our mother's. We were all bound up in grief, and because of our Englishness, had fewer ways to deal with it. We might have had Italian summers of passion and excitement and shouting and wild displays of childish emotions, but when it came to the rites and rituals of life, we reverted to type.

I felt most sorry for Paola, who was unaccompanied, even though we were all there with her, her siblings. John should have been there and I felt angry at him for being overworked. Even though it was something I envied in a way, being so monstrously and noticeably unemployed myself. I envied anyone with any sort of an income, especially Brod and Suzanna, who didn't have a worry in the world. Truthfully speaking, Harriet and I deserved the largest chunk out of Mama's will, if the world was anything like a fair place. We cared for her so well. We spent so much in airfares and things while she was unwell. Back and forth, back and forth.

I shook my head in an effort to stall extreme annoyance. Well, fairness was most likely going to be the outcome, so how could I expect more? But we sorely needed it. I contained irritation and aimed it in my heart at Paola's husband. Undeniably – work was not a good enough excuse to allow one's wife to travel to Italy alone all the way from Melbourne, and to live through what could be easily one of life's most difficult four days. A week. Whatever.

Harriet would not have dreamt of leaving me to deal with my mother's funeral on my own. We do things together, my wife and I. How peculiar to see John and Paola go about things in such a different way. Even Lewis, quiet and taciturn as he was, was Suzanna's shadow, a loyal and true partner if ever there was one. I bet she would not have been half as successful without him.

I was honestly also a bit irate at Suzanna for asking so many questions about where this item and that object were. How was I to know what happened to the sideboard or bookcase or whatever the large piece of furniture was called?

She did come down to the kitchen the night before the funeral, breathless, as if she had gone through the entire house, room by room by room, seeking things she remembered.

I wanted to confront her, scold her for thinking only about material things at such a time, but I bit my lip and kept silent. I had to say something, though. 'Shall I put the kettle on?'

She took three deep breaths. 'Yes, Nigel. Do. Please.' Quite out of breath. 'If you counted the number of little flights of stairs and steps and staircases and whatnot in this house... phew.'

'A hundred and ...'

' ... thirty-one!' She remembered.

We would all, as children, play hide-and-seek, various hiding games, seeking games, shouting and silent games all through the house. One of the things we surely knew was the number of steps in the places. *Su e giù, su e giù,* we would chant, as Matilde had taught us.

'Up and down,' she said, taking a seat at the big red table. 'Down and up.'

I didn't ask whether she had been in every single room, because it was the kind of interrogation she expected, so I held back, spiteful, leaving it to her to state. She would not enter the rooms we were all occupying while we were there, anyway.

'So what do you think will be in the will tomorrow, Nigel?'

I poured hot water into the big brown teapot, which steamed up my glasses, and said nothing.

She waited.

'I was more ... I'm more anxious and nervous

about the funeral, Suzanna.' There. I said it pointedly, to make her feel a bit like she ought to, rather than worrying about sideboards and carpets and what we would all do about selling the house.

'I'm trying not to think about tomorrow.' Her voice was muted in the large kitchen. 'I'm trying ...'

What was she trying to do – avoid the emotion? Postpone it? This was not what Suzanna was like. As a young person she confronted people, stared them in the eye. Demanded what she wanted. Asked what she wanted to know. Loudly.

'Tomorrow will be over before we know it. It might feel like the longest day in our lives, but it's something...'

'I know what it is, Nigel. I'm not sixteen, you know! And I have been to a number of funerals. We have all lost friends, and parents of friends, and colleagues ... oh, I have had my share of funerals.'

'None of them like this one.'

She was silent for a minute, pulling the cup and saucer I slid towards her and clinking the teaspoon against the cup. 'No, true. None of them as ... significant.'

'Or emotional.'

'How many people do you think will be there?'

'Certainly not more than about thirty. I think there are some older people down at San Girolamo who remember her well, and of course there will always be the steadfast churchgoer or two.'

'Or six.'

'Yes, who appear at every ceremony or mass or whatever, simply because it's on.'

'So we'll have the village set there as well.'

'No doubt. Do you want a biscuit with your tea?'

She made a face. 'I don't eat biscuits! It's amazing, Nigel – I am fifty-three, and yet you guys treat me like I was still six or ten or thirteen. I might have eaten the odd biscuit Matilde baked when I was in ankle socks ... but a lot of water has gone under the bridge.'

I didn't say, *You're fifty-five Suzanna*. I said instead, 'And I might have collected anything and everything bearing a slight resemblance to a stamp when I was twelve, but I don't any more.'

'There you are!'

'And I used to have everything pointed out to me because I was the youngest, Suzanna, but I can see things quite plainly for myself now.' I formed my hands into binoculars, like a little kid, and ogled around the kitchen. A controlled effort, to keep irritation in check.

She laughed at that point. She took a dainty sip of the tea I made her and laughed again. 'You'll always be the youngest, Nigel.'

It was my turn to smile.

'Now tell me what's eating you.'

Oh lord – I was not about to tell her I'd been made redundant and having bills and things to pay that came up to my eyeballs.

And she saw I was not going to disclose what was eating me to her. Not then. Not ever.

'Missing Mama, I guess. This is certainly not the best reason to have a family reunion, and even though Harriet and I and the children lived here when she was ill and ... and ... It's still not comfortable or easy.'

'No, it couldn't be. Don't think we blame you for things not being where we thought they'd always be, though, Nigel.'

'Blame me?'

'I can't find the bookcase!'

'Oh?' I had to take a deep breath to stay calm. She was blaming me.

'It wasn't in any of those partially-renovated bedrooms in the wing. It would have been beautifully dry there. I can't remember its condition.'

'Did it have a deep bottom drawer which ...?'

'Yes. It did.' She sipped tea. 'Look. Forget about it. Now all we need to find out is what's eating Brod. I don't want to be the one to ask him.'

'It had all those records in it, remember? Papa's record collection. I'd give my right arm for them, today. Never gave it a thought when I was young. We're music mad in my family – the kids both play. We have classical music in our blood. Harriet's grandmother was a concert pianist. I wonder where all those records went, Suzanna – but stuff is like that. It goes. Like the bookcase. Like the one dining room chair. Like the curtains someone mentioned. Stuff vanishes.'

'Do you think we should have been more ... or perhaps Mama should have ...? I don't know!' She huffed anger through her nostrils and took off on heels clattering on the old tiles.

Brod

A missing painting

Grant could be quite an amazing person. He was touched and worried about Paola, who was the only sibling there without a partner. She was quite as detached as our nephew Tad, who was only there for a while at the church, and disappeared afterwards. We wondered what and where the boy ate and how Harriet and Nigel managed his solitariness. If they thought it needed management at all. I guessed I would never understand children, although I did – as a youngster – occasionally go through phases I could liken to Tad's behaviour. It was very probable this attitude thing of his was a phase too. My brother didn't seem too worried about his son. He seemed burdened by something else.

'I walked out in the rain to Paola,' Grant said, 'who was drifting out there, distressed, in the long wet grass, without an umbrella or anything. There were two old raincoats on a rail, so I put one on, and took the other out to her.'

'Oh, Grant – that was nice.' We walked down one of the steep narrow streets of Fiesole, which were made of steps. There was a break in the very changeable Fiesole weather which buoyed us; no need for an umbrella now. Window boxes full of flowers, high yellow walls, green-painted shutters and wrought iron balconies surrounded us. If we'd been tourists, it would have been hard to distinguish the *pensione* we were staying at from other large yellow houses.

I wondered how long the rain would hold off, but the strip of sky above us, at least, was a shade of pleasant blue. It was unusual to be in Fiesole at such a wet and chilly time of the year.

Grant walked along with his hands in his jeans pockets, looking at his feet as we descended one stepped street. 'Brod, her husband's left her. John … is it John?'

I stopped, gaped, and held my breath for a moment. This was incredible news.

'… immediately before she flew out from Melbourne.'

Two surprises in two breaths. 'Incredible!' Of all the relationships in the family, Paola and John's used to seem to me to be strongest. 'Did she say why?' Paola had chosen to confide in Grant – a perfect stranger – which was even more atypical of her.

'He met someone.'

I could imagine Paola's sarcastic voice and the way she would have pulled her mouth to utter those words. 'What – so you walked in the rain and …'

'It was awful ... but good – you know what I mean? Do you know that rare instance when the time is right for someone to talk? I felt so flattered to be confided in, and by your big sister of all people. She stood and spilled it all out. How he told her before he jumped in a taxi to fly to Brisbane.'

'Goodness. She must still be smarting from it all. I have to ... should I? Should I talk to her? I think I should. Did she ask you not to tell me, or anything?' I stopped in front of a sharp corner as two girls on scooters whizzed past.

'No. She seemed relieved to get it off her chest. We both got quite damp in the rain. We returned and put the raincoats back, and she went in to pour us two glasses of the old cellared wine, and we sat in the room where you said you used to sit with your mother.'

I could see Grant there, with Paola.

'She's very nice, Brod.'

'Of course she is.'

'No ... come on. You know what I mean. I first thought she was sullen and sarcastic ... and prim. Now I know she had reason.'

I could not disagree. 'Paola ... she's ... oh, poor Paola. You know, she's the oldest, the wisest, and has a fabulous memory. She remembers stuff from when she was four, and six, and fifteen.'

'She says it's a curse, and doesn't mean it as a joke.'

I agreed. 'She was always a sombre and serious type. Not given to joking.'

Grant moved to face me. 'She can be bitingly ... intelligently ... funny. I mean her humour is dry.'

'Humour!' But I saw what he meant. I thought of something. 'Grant ... you didn't tell her – you didn't return the favour and confide in her, did you?'

'Well ...'

'Oh, Grant. There was no need. We'll sort it out ourselves.' I hoped my voice didn't whine, but I was annoyed.

He folded his arms. 'I felt there was need. We found something, on a brief rainy walk. We talked. Properly, honestly, you know – no holding back. Besides, I wanted to get it off my chest.'

'Paola would have thought you were telling tales. On me.'

He huffed, annoyed with me. Annoyed and exasperated with me. 'Ah! Huh!'

'Grant.'

'Um – I asked her if she thought it was too old to think of adopting an infant at ... if ... when one is over fifty. I am fifty-eight, Brod. This is about me, too.'

I didn't think Paola was the ideal person to ask, having no children of her own, and being my big sister. I said as much, and he must have seen the displeasure on my face. 'So what did she have to say?'

'She's very nice, you know.'

'You said that before.'

'She pointed out the fact we'd be pushing seventy when the child was in high school, if we started now.'

I blinked.

'And you have to admit we never thought of it in such a ... a time frame. We'd be drained. On our last legs. I'd be exhausted. I don't think I can push myself that far, Brod. I mean – we have such a nice free life now ...'

'Doing what we want.'

'Mm.'

'Let's not talk about it to anyone else, shall we? No more. Until we finally resolve the ... the situation, I mean. The decision. The pros and cons. Certainly not here, not now. Not with *my family*.'

'Paola ... it seemed to take her mind off her own problems.'

'Did she say anything else?'

'She talked about a missing painting.'

I rolled my eyes and thanked goodness we could change the subject. 'Lots has gone missing. We all noticed. It gets on Suzanna's nerves. Nigel doesn't say anything, even if he and Harriet notice, or even know where some things have ended up. I tend not to register such things. Things, you know, Grant ... *things*. Everything can be replaced.'

'Not everything, according to your big sister. She said something about an umbrella painting, which used to hang in the drawing room.'

'Oh lord – yes. *Ombrelli a Santa Maria*.' The fabulous painting we all had imprinted into our minds as children was suddenly there, in my mind's eye. 'Basile painted it.'

'Who?'

'Basile – he was ... like a family friend. I wonder what happened to him.' Remembering Basile was like a strange flash from a forgotten part of my childhood. How could I forget Basile? What did I remember of him? He had a bright, lean face. His English was good; he had travelled the world, and his art was quite distinctive. Mama had met him at some artistic convention – goodness knew where. We did not know her exact movements when we were all away at school.

Grant and I got in the car and drove to Via Faentina, where there was a little restaurant I liked. A quick but relaxed lunch was what we needed, away from the big house for a while, and it was important to show Grant the rest of Fiesole.

I could not get the painting out of my mind, even when we sat at a small table. 'It was special. All these coloured open umbrellas, leading to a church. Santa Maria. Important – but I don't know why. Did Paola say anything more? Does she know if Basile ever took off as a painter?'

'She described it so minutely, so cleverly. I could see it ... in the rain. Me and your sister, standing there, getting very nearly drenched, and I could see all the coloured umbrellas, slick with rain, all grouped together, with the church in the background, like molten gold, she said.'

'Yes. Yes!' I remembered. The objects in our childhood which formed the stage backdrop of our little dramas disappeared with time. Yet when they were there, they were possibly what formed our opinions, taste, likes and dislikes. What we thought of art and love. What we adored about music. What we chose to read. The thumb of culture, around which a whole life's choices were wound, like a length of yarn. Like the thumb, influences were withdrawn and disappeared, leaving only what they formed. A weirdly-wound ball of impressions.

When we remembered them, we recalled the

accompanying events. The people. Basile – what was his last name? He was a violinist as well as an artist. He played with a number of famous orchestras. Yes, Basile Sottalbero. Tall, thin, patient and very good-looking. Our Renaissance man. 'He taught us about ... who was the poet? Ah – Leopardi, or someone similar.' I knew nothing about where he could be, or why he had disappeared out of our lives.

'Shall we?' Grant held up a menu.

'This trip is turning into a pilgrimage, Grant. I'm sorry if ...'

He leaned forward suddenly and grabbed me by the upper arm. 'Brod, I love it. I never had this. It's brilliant. Your family's ... I don't know ... they're real. All memories, and questions, and quarrels and ... I don't know ... you guys don't even know how much you love each other.'

I lowered my head. We were all ageing. We didn't love each other when we were youngsters. How could we now? What did Grant see that I didn't? 'Rubbish, Grant.'

'Rubbish, then.' He let go of my arm. 'You know each other so well.' He took up a fork and ate his salad.

'We think we know each other – but it's only what we remember of adolescent moods, silly behaviour, tantrums, childish habits. We've all changed. Mostly, we've changed because of the people we've chosen to live with.'

He smiled.

'Yes – you've changed me a bit, Grant. I used to be so ... slapdash. So bland.'

He looked up. 'Hmm. You still wear terrible

sweaters.'

I pulled a face at him.

Later, much later, after a mostly silent main course, he broke into his round brittle torta, which was covered in raspberry juice. 'You treat each other like you're all still teenagers. It's hilarious.'

I didn't think it was funny. It was devastatingly sad.

Suzanna

Not always alone

I watched my twin and his partner. They sat on either side of the fireplace in the front sitting room, where Mama would gather us sometimes, on very hot afternoons, for a bit of quiet reading. I didn't think I had ever seen the fireplace working, and yet Brod got it to burn nicely, with a few dry logs he brought up from somewhere.

The cosy scene was not perfect. They had evidently had words. Brod glared at Grant, and Grant stuck his tongue out at him. So they were all right, I supposed. Just like Mama was all right with us when we had annoyed her. She'd read to us, to calm us down. How boring it was some of those long afternoons!

And how warm and sticky! She would place two pedestal fans at opposite ends of the room, hoist her feet onto a footstool, read aloud out of some book or other – almost certainly Enid Blyton, and later Agatha Christie or the English translations of the Maigret novels – and we would either all drop off for a nap where we lay on the rug around her, or wander off. Brod had a quiet game – a habit – of tracing the rug pattern with his fingers, following the design from end to end, and all along the border. He would listen to the reading and trace, trace, with a frown of concentration between his eyebrows. He was crazy about those rugs. When he doodled, he drew a corner of the library rug!

And yes, now Brod mentioned it to me, I did remember the big umbrella painting between the two front windows. Gone. A little one now hung in its place. Paola wasn't the only one who remembered our childhood idiosyncrasies. Now it was mentioned, I remembered the musty smell of wood and paper and dust whenever I hid in the bottom drawer of the big beautiful bookcase in the hall. There was no danger of it tipping forward with my weight, little thing that I was. Besides, it was a substantial, stable piece of furniture, much higher than a man, made of mahogany and satinwood. What a magnificent thing it was! I would run fingers along the marquetry, jump in the drawer, wait to be found, and run back to this room laughing and shouting afterwards, at whichever of my siblings had won the game.

It was so cold in there now! I moved closer to the fire. My brother and Grant rose, and invited me for a walk down to the rubble wall, but I preferred to stay, not to ruin my shoes, so I did, and studied the place; the heavy brocade curtains, which needed cleaning, and on the wall between the windows, the small picture I did not remember. Or maybe I did. It might have hung in one of the refurbished rooms Papa wanted to fill with paying guests. Such dreamy schemes, he had – I loved them all. I learned from him what I wanted to do when I grew up. Buy and sell properties and businesses. Make money!

I also learned I wanted to sail – a bit from him, but mostly later. He taught me to identify what I wanted, and how I should go about getting it. Now Lewis and I were so close to our big dream; getting a yacht and sailing the Mediterranean. Mama's bequest would help enormously. It was practically in the bag!

I expected Lewis to join me for a·bit of quiet time to ourselves, but Paola came in with a book, no doubt searching for a quiet place to read. We still hadn't discussed the will, and I wasn't about to broach the subject with my older sister, even though her face appeared serene now, much calmer than when we all arrived a few days ago. The pressure and anticipation about the funeral and the reading of the will were gone. Our mother was at rest, at last! We could all now exchange memories and stories without fear our guilt or fear or greed would be exposed. I believed they all did find me greedy, grasping, materialistic ... and I simply was a bit more realistic than most!

But Lewis would tell anyone it was what kept me motivated. It was hardly believable, was it? Lewis rarely spoke, and especially not to my family.

I did catch him sitting at one end of the long table with Lori, though. They had a bottle of something nice and two really tiny stemmed glasses. Lori had magicked up a little plate of biscuits, which very much resembled the ones Matilde used to make.

I meant to ask her where she got them, to make conversation, but something drew me to the front sitting room, and there I sat for a while with Paola, talking about when we were all in our teens. Papa had been dead a few years, and we had only recently got used to having our summers without him.

'The wall gods ... do you remember trying to copy them on squared graph paper? Do you remember spilling poster paint on the hall floor?'

I didn't. Paola went into a host of more details about finding fossils in the rubble wall, about wishing for a pool, about our matching swimming suits one summer, and the new straw hats we bought at the Sunday market.

'I simply don't remember, Paola.'

'You must remember winters, and school, better.'

'Mama had some dreadful winters in Cornwall, getting used to being alone.'

'She wasn't always alone, Suzanna.'

'No – I remember the winter Nigel got pneumonia, and he had to be collected from school. He was sick a long time. There was the winter I broke my leg.'

Paola held up a finger. 'Yes, I think it was the year, and the following winter ... no, the winter after. Do you remember how she phoned us from somewhere else?'

'No. What – phoned from somewhere else in England?'

She dog-eared a page and closed the book. I saw her feet rested on the very same footstool Mama had used all those years ago. It was rush-woven, with a small tapestry cushion on top. It was comforting. I could also smell something delicious from Nigel's kitchen, but sat back and waited for Paola's memories to kick in. How efficient her brain was!

'From Belgium, actually.'

'Belgium!'

'Don't you remember? We took the call together, you and I, in the bursar's office, up in the college building. Her voice was loud and faraway-sounding, and she felt happy and ... light-hearted.'

I had only a dim memory, if I could call it a memory. 'And?'

'And she was in France and Belgium, on a driving trip with Basile.'

'Bas... oh my goodness. Do I remember someone called Basile?'

Paola tilted her head. 'Of course you do. I hope you do.'

'And you think they had a – a thing? Mama would never do such a thing.'

A furrow appeared on the bridge of Paola's nose. 'Why ever not? She was a normal woman. Basile was a lovely man. Papa had been dead for years. Can you conceive of the emptiness, the loneliness? Think of yourself in your late forties, or the age she was at the time.'

I sat up. 'Well – I'm in my very early fifties now!'

'You're fifty-five, Suzanna. But it's exactly what I mean. So what if she had a thing with Basile?'

I shrugged. 'So what happened? Why wasn't he here in the summer, then?'

She leaned forward, her sudden movement

knocking the book off the chair arm to the floor. She ignored it. 'He was. He was. Try to remember – he had two rooms at the back of the wing. The rust-coloured room, remember? And they put a desk and his easels and paints and things in the next room, and he had the bathroom with the enormous drippy showerhead. The one Donato had to fix over and over again.'

'Paola – you're making it up. No one remembers so many details about stuff that happened like four decades ago!'

'Not four decades.'

'Mama wasn't like that.'

'Like what? She wasn't a nun, I can tell you.'

I paused. 'So what happened to Basile?'

There was a long pause. 'How on earth would I know? I can only remember things I was there to see, or things I was told. Or things I heard. I can't remember things I never knew.'

'But...'

'It must have ended. Relationships end.'

I rose and moved to the window, and saw the rain had stopped and some beautiful watery sunshine bathed the trees and rooftops between the house and the shimmering church tower in the distance.

'Look at the cathedral ... everything seems so much smaller to an adult, doesn't it? It seemed gigantic and so high when we were children.' I stepped into the room. 'Not all relationships end, Paola.'

'They do,' she said quickly. She seemed to form one square brown entity in that large armchair.

'Death, or misadventure, or infidelity, or boredom, or money, or accident, or folly, or chance ... or one of the pair could meet someone – and some couples stay together even though the relationship's shot to bits.'

'Goodness. You do sound ...'

'Angry? I am. I am angry. John's left me, Suzanna.'

'Oh Paola.' What a surprise for her to blurt it out in such a way! I didn't want to sound sorry for her. She did seem strong and confident, more confident than when we all arrived.

'*Oh Paola* indeed,' she said with a woeful smile. A mock woeful smile.

'So you're okay?'

She reached down for the book on the rug, put it in her lap and sat back. Her long sigh was loud in the room. 'I'm okay.'

I was not about to say anything about marriage or children or money. What could I say? What a thing! 'I guess the will ...'

She held up a hand. 'You and I know the will was perfect, Suzanna. Perfect. Absolutely right. Mama could not have got it more right.'

I had to agree. 'So you're happy. Are you happy?'

'With the will? Yes, of course. So are you. You can't deny it. It's all going to work so well. All we have to do is sign the all-important *dichiarazione di successione* ...'

'The acceptance of the will, yes – and so? I guess we'll sign.' Was it so easy? The notary made it sound more complicated than it needed to be.

'Well yes – you and me. But do you think Nigel and Brod are as content as we are?

She sat forward again, craning her neck, looking like she was going to say something confidential. It was so unlike her I went back to my chair and leaned forward in the same way. 'What?'

'Nigel and Harriet – I thought their marriage was ... you know, in trouble.'

'Good heavens – no! Could it be?'

'Well, no. I think I thought so because of my own ... well, listen – John had only sprung it on me very recently, and I saw everything through the fog of my anger. No – no. They're okay, I think, but something is definitely bothering them. Both of them, and I think I know what it is.'

'One of the children ...?'

She laughed. 'They couldn't ask for nicer kids. Do you remember how we all heartily disapproved of the way ... you know, their parenting style?'

So it wasn't Lori or Tad worrying our little brother and his wife.

'I think it's to do with money.'

I raised my eyes toward the cracked ceiling. 'Well. Well, then – the will might have fixed such matters for them.'

'After it all goes through. Even if we sign this week, it will take a while. I agree though – didn't you see Nigel's face after the reading?'

I laughed. 'I'm not the one who checks everyone's expression ... and remembers it years afterwards, Paola! It's what you do, not me!'

She didn't take offense. 'He was beaming. He looked like the weight of the world had suddenly dropped off his shoulders.'

'Aha. I still can't get over how you remember things. The painting! Basile – wow! Was he tall and a bit pale and ...'

'He smoked funny fat cigars. He would wheel a wide canvas out on an easel, to the rubble wall. He'd prop it just so. He would set up a market umbrella, and he'd stay there for literally hours. Landscapes, panoramic landscapes. And Fiesole streetscapes.'

'You watched him.'

'Of course I watched him.'

'Did he talk ...'

'He taught me to sketch a little. He taught me about distances.'

I didn't understand. 'Distances?'

'Between objects.'

I laughed, because I still didn't see what she meant. Why didn't I remember any of this? I barely remembered the man. 'How many summers was he here?'

'Four.'

'You sound so sure. How can you be so sure? It's simply ages ago!'

Paola held the book to her chest, with shoulders curled inward, in a self-protective huddle. Her eyes went darker. 'I loved him too, Suzanna.' There was something in her voice, something precluding a response; which silenced everything else.

I heard a motor scooter in the distance, somewhere on the terraced streets of Fiesole. I heard a distant church bell. I heard my sister breathing. Her face was a mask of remorse. She regretted something.

'I'm sorry I told you now. I'm sorry I said anything. It was important to me. What was I? Sixteen?' She closed her eyes. Her lips were pressed together, white.

'I won't tell ...'

And suddenly she was weeping, into her bunched shawl, which she pulled from her shoulders roughly, angrily. She wept audibly, with copious tears wetting and staining the shawl. No more words, only strangled sobs which sounded desperately sad. Oh, Paola!

I placed a hand on her shoulder, and she did not shrug it off. So I pulled her to her feet and embraced her, my older sister, and she sobbed on my shoulder. Oh – I felt it in her; it was all the resentment about John, and all the memories of Basile, rolled into the aftermath of the funeral.

I caught my breath, and felt my chest crowd with emotion.

'Don't you cry too,' she mumbled. There was a small repressed laugh. 'How sad we are. How miserably, stupidly, angrily, terrifyingly sad.' She wiped her face on the shawl, stood back and sniffed. 'Better now. Thank you.'

I watched her leave the sitting room, back straight, book hugged to her chest, ruined shawl trailing behind her.

Five minutes. It took five minutes for me to take it in. Paola; strong, unflappable, serious, solemn Paola, had loved an older man, a family friend. Our mother's lover. So many years ago. It could have meant everything to her in those early years.

I only loved – liked – funny Italian village boys who whistled at me when I cycled down to the ice cream shop in my shorts. I didn't even remember any of their names. I smoked cigarettes on corners, listened to Italian pop songs blaring from tiny cafés, cycled frantically fast homeward, uphill all the way, with my siblings, and went back to school in September, in a navy blue gym slip, without a backward thought.

I never had an inkling of what Paola thought or felt. Ever. We were so different. Years apart in age. And now I felt protective of her, did I? She appeared crushed and vulnerable. Almost old and frail when she wept like she did, on my shoulder. Damn and blast John. Silly man! She loved him and he let her down.

Someone put their head in the door. It was Lori. 'Auntie Suzanna – I think I've kept you two apart long enough. I need to practise now.'

'What a lovely smile, darling. Yes – off you go. What did you talk about for such a long time? I didn't think Lewis had so much to ... discuss!'

She came part of the way into the room and lowered her voice. 'It's so sweet. All he talks about is you.'

Brod

Adoption

The strange thing about spending a week with one's siblings after so many years was the fundamental change one witnessed. The false impression they remained the same people one knew as a child is ingrained, well entrenched, until one spent enough time talking and watching. They were in fact nothing like the children they used to be. Nothing.

Suzanna, for one, was not as mercenary or selfish as she was as a teenager. Still as self-conscious about her appearance, however. Nigel was a lot more cagey and secretive, but his tantrums – not surprisingly – were somehow not as frequent. I still kept waiting for one. Paola – I didn't know about Paola. All we noticed was her capacity to recreate scenes and snatches of our childhood we had long forgotten. I thought we all feared what she remembered. She was more terse and grumpy, if anything. The end of a marriage could do strange things to a woman, I supposed. And Mama's funeral affected us all.

And what about me? I was more jumpy. More prone to confusion, more emotional, at fifty-five. I messed up my reading in the church. I hardly made it all the way through without swallowing and wincing. It would have been so embarrassing to break down mid-sentence. I didn't dare make eye contact with Grant. He must have held his breath the entire time. He did say, earlier, when I showed him the readings Nigel had chosen, that mine was far too long. I did add Mama had left written instructions. He was sure Nigel had added to the pieces; marked out longer sections from the works listed.

The music affected me more than I could say. Days passed now and I was less numb, so the effect started to seep into me. My throat always seized to *Abide with me*. To have it sung at one's mother's funeral was intolerable. It still cycled through my head. I wondered what the Italian guests thought of it all.

And through the singing, and the whole thing, with tears brimming, I wondered whether Grant prayed. It can happen when one finds oneself in a church. I know for certain he's not the type – he doesn't believe in much, but I imagined him praying for me to change my mind about adopting.

Now what put a baby in my head? I have no idea, but I had watched any number of celebrities – gay or not – with their adopted children, and I suddenly got this yen to be a parent. How perfect it could all be. Grant's eyes were wide with disbelief when I mentioned it.

'You must be joking.'

'I'm perfectly serious.'

He gradually, over weeks, built up an argument in favour of not changing things, until we faced each other on this Fiesole funeral trip, where he seemed to have all his excuses lined up in a row. 'I don't think we'd make ideal parents – do you? We're so random. Topsy-turvy and all over the place.'

It was rubbish, of course. We were both quite organized and clean and tidy. 'We are not.'

'We travel a lot.'

'Children aren't cartons of raw eggs, Grant – they can travel. They ... they grow. I mean ... Lori and Tad!'

'I do see them. I imagine it took a fortune to raise them.'

I smiled. 'It did, actually. Nigel was always grumbling about bills and things. Dentists, trips, school fees ... he never stopped.' I stopped my mouth with my hand. I should have spoken positively. Foolish, silly; mindlessly sabotaging my own arguments. 'But look at all the ...'

'Joy? Happiness? I'd rather be an uncle. So would you, Brod. I don't see you avidly interested in your nephew and niece.'

'What are you saying?'

He spread his fingers and grimaced. 'It's not like you're so interested in children. It's ... it can be ... it is momentous. I mean, difficult. Almost impossible. A mammoth task. Never-ending. Not something you try for *a while*. It's a forever commitment. Tremendous – I'm not sure I'm cut out for all the complication.'

'How many times have we had this conversation?'

He laughed and hurried his pace. 'Every time we have free time to stop and draw breath. We are two very busy people, Brod.'

'Mm – I know.'

'I can't see you carrying a baby capsule or whatever it's called in to the child-minding centre ... or whatever it's called ... at your bank in the commercial centre of Manchester. Or the Brussels branch, where you go four or more times a year.'

'Shall we choose to enjoy this break now?' Apologetic. I felt sorry for raking it all up again. Besides, quite frankly, I was not so sure any longer. It was obvious now what caused my confusion.

Nigel

Harriet is told

I chopped and diced vegetables without a real plan in mind. Soup? A stew? What was I doing? Someone said we should all troop down to a restaurant for one of the last nights; so what was I doing preparing so many things? The kitchen table groaned with bowls of prepared vegetables.

'We bought too much, Nige.'

'Harriet honey, we need to empty the fridge. It's a shame to throw out such a lot of stuff.'

'So have we all sorted out whether we're staying in or going out for dinner?'

'Brod and Grant would like to go out.'

'Tonight or tomorrow? Paola too?' Harriet put the heels of both hands on the table and leaned forward. I could see she held herself in check and spoke through a stiff pair of lips. 'Your big sister is acting ... seventeen. No – seventy. I've never ... what is it? Hormones? Menopause? Age? Stubbornness?'

I had to step back and take a breath before answering, or something I regretted might escape my own lips. Paola could be so condescending she was capable of putting anyone into a frozen moment of rage. When she asked if anything by Palestrina would be played at the funeral, it was a dig at me, but also a slur on Mama's taste in music. I was not about to do the same to her. As a boy, I would have hidden one of her skates, or snipped off one of her bathing suit straps. I'd grown out of petty juvenile revenge. Best to say nothing.

'Come on, Nige – surely you're not reaching for an excuse for her? She marched past me in the passage. She hardly blinked. Why doesn't she talk to me? It would only be civil.'

'Sit down, Harriet.' I reached for the kettle.

'When you start boiling kettles and filling teapots, Nigel Larkin, I know there's something meaningful going on. What's happened now?'

I smiled at my wife. At least she conceded there was something she didn't know. 'You're impatient, that's all. Sit down and open this tin. It's got *cantuccini* in it.'

'I've put on a couple of pounds since we've been here this time.'

'We need to take a walk and go up and down those winding lanes and steep stepped streets.' I had to smile. She was quite easy to placate.

Nibbling at one of the almond biscotti, she was now completely calmed. 'Okay. Now tell me what's wrong with Paola.'

'John was getting ready to go on a conference in Queensland ... or somewhere, and ...'

'Oh goodness. Is he all right?'

'He left.'

'What?'

'He's left the marriage, just like that – and told her at the front gate, with a taxi waiting.'

Harriet swallowed the last of the biscuit, and hooked her dark hair behind her ears. 'You're joking. Who told you this? Poor Paola. No wonder she's as rigid as a ... and she had to get through the funeral and all the rest, all on her own.'

I poured hot water onto three spoons of tea leaves. The scent filled the room. 'She's a bit in awe of you, I think.'

'Of me – rubbish. I mean ...' Her eyes grew wide. 'Even Lewis is ... '

I knew what she meant. 'Only Lewis can be Lewis.'

'He's behind Suzanna all the way, and at least nods and smiles before he runs away from us.'

I tidied away the peel, still wondering what to do with the diced vegetables. 'Yes. He's lovely to Suzanna, which is what matters. He's not the pancake-making type, or the chatty type, but he's fine.'

'They never had kids, so they're not like us, Nige. We've had to rally together ...'

'... even if only to pay the bloody bills.'

'Ha!'

'So cut Paola some slack, eh?'

My wife shook her head apologetically. 'What is Paola going to do?' But her eyes were somehow full of a feminine knowing. 'Oh, gosh ... the will surely worked out in her favour, if what I ...'

'I don't know.' It had worked so well in our favour I wasn't willing to discuss it with any of my siblings yet. There was still the acceptance document to sign. Were we all putting off discussing it, for fear of upsetting such a fine balance? Mama had thought it out so well it would be a pity to destroy it all with a pointless heated argument. 'I don't know what Paola intends to do.'

'She's always been secretive and sort of quiet and brooding, though – hasn't she?'

'She's not like you, Harriet – you're pretty forthright and blunt.'

Her chin dropped. 'Oh – thank you very much.'

'Well – you are. I always know where I stand with you.'

She was mollified. 'At least, it's something. At least you haven't left me ... in the front garden, with a taxi meter running. Did he give a reason? Damn John. What was he *thinking?*'

'Couldn't have thought very much about anything, could he? Paola said he met someone.'

'Met someone? At sixty-two or how old he is? Met someone! After twenty-something years with your sister. Or nearly thirty ... or whatever! And there I was thinking they had the best relationship of all.'

It was my turn to thank her very much.

'You know what I mean, Nige. They never had trumpet lessons to argue over, or teeth, or blazers, or the bloody phone-and-internet bill. Or the alternator on the clapped-out car.'

We laughed together in the same way. I reached for a biscuit and passed her a mug. She had already eaten two.

'Leave us a biscuit, all right?'

She laughed again.

'This reminds me of when I'd sit down here with Mama, me and her alone together. She would tap a finger on my door and say *Nigel, pancakes*, so no one else could hear, and we'd sit here gorging ourselves and talking.' I dropped my head and squeezed my eyes shut for a second. Being the youngest, and having least memories of my father, I supposed Mama paid special attention to me and my tantrums and demands. 'I could be pretty ghastly as a child.'

'You haven't changed much.' Her brilliant smile lit up the kitchen.

Paola

A few changes

I drove down to Prato on my own, leaving the other three gathered on the back terrace, in the sun. They had pulled some kitchen chairs out there, and a small table, and Harriet brought a tray laden with things.

I was pleased to have the zippy little rental at my disposal, over the moon about the will, but still wondered how I would manage the obvious negotiation required, to get specifically what I wanted from the bequest. Also, importantly, without telling anyone about my lotto win. I could imagine Harriet's face if she got to know about the events crowding the days around Mama's death. I can imagine her mouth forming the words, *What? I don't believe it. It can't be true.*

But it was. I was coming to terms with it all, but I must have appeared pale and stunned to her that first day, when I climbed out of the car and she asked why John was not with me. Stunned, numb, and still in a state of shock. Still awed by the amount of money in my bank account. Still dazed, trying to get used to the fact Mama was no more. It was more than one person could handle. Now I had the will to consider.

Mama did it all very cleverly, I had to admit. I had to admire her retention of brain power, fairness, intellect, control; everything we remembered her for. She did it all in a way I would have liked to run my life. I never had four children – and I was never a widow. Neither did I have houses in two places. Our lives were nowhere near the same. I still dearly wished for what she had, however, for years. Something ineffable – but she had it. For years going about knowing I had a less crowded life, more freedom, was what I thought was most satisfying. I supposed it was, of course.

No – what was I thinking? I went for years wanting what she had – a house crowded with the laughter of children. Which never came.

The bitterness rising as I wound down to Prato, though, was a new brand of resentment brought on by something other than my own causes. I did not create my current predicament. I wasn't the one who chose to be suddenly single and very nearly lost.

I had to deal with it, though. I had to handle it all with some sort of calm integrity. Not my words. Funnily enough, it was Harriet who, to my surprise, provided the words. After I stormed past her a couple of times, wanting to stick a Neptune trident tine in her eye, and also in one of Nigel's, she stopped me, right in front of the big windows near the brown armchair Mama would sit in when she came in from the garden, her shoes caked with soil. I was in the dark about what my sister-in-law wanted, but I simply could not be rude. It was too late in life for my wall god to come to the rescue.

'Paola. Nigel's told me. I won't say I'm sorry, because no one's been hurt or killed or anything.' She paused, in a breathless gap in which she tried to gauge my reaction.

I gave none.

'I know you will cope, with your amazing calm integrity.'

Surprise kept me on the spot, with sunshine in my eyes, with my mouth open. I had to look her in the eye and thank her. 'I couldn't say anything, Harriet, when I drove up the first day, and you asked about John. I couldn't speak about him. I was completely ... absolutely ... livid.'

She gave a half-smile. What did she know about wretched anger? What could she possibly know about paralytic fury?

I went on. 'And yes – I have a sort of plan. Well – I'm forming a plan, and it feels good to be able to do things independently.'

'You of all people ... of course. You have your writing and your wonderful world. Solitary, you can be, integral, successful. You should know you are envied by many.' And she walked off towards the kitchen, and her husband and children.

Tad had reappeared from somewhere, still in his threadbare blazer, which he apparently could not bring himself to abandon, and Lori was talking about the festival in Florence again.

I was transfixed to the spot. My wonderful

world, she called it. This was how she regarded what I did. Years went by and we fixed in our minds what others might think of us. We were so often wrong.

I was wrong about Harriet. She was not supercilious and arrogant. She seemed a touch envious and admired my life as a writer. I had never thought of myself as calm, or integral. Or solitary and successful – but I could be so. If I appeared so to her, there had to be an element of truth in it. We would never see eye to eye about life, and we could never be real friends, but I could not dismiss her out of hand.

Calm and integral. Hah! I drove downhill to the Via Sestese and took it all the way into Prato. The traffic was quite incredible. I had to keep my head. The address the notary supplied did not appear to be a hospice or home. It was not easy to find. I should not have volunteered to be the first to visit Matilde, after all, and would have done better to wait until someone else had found the place and could give me directions. Driving on the right was not what I would have called comfortable, and with no one else in the car, I felt on edge and constantly scared something would happen. If driving was on the right, did one give way to the left? Hm. Give way – Italian drivers did not *give way*. There was not enough room on the road, for a start.

Everything made me jump. Come on. I had driven in Europe so much in the past. Was this a sign of age? Was I growing old? Even one instance of a back wheel riding the curb rendered me shaky.

'Concentrate!' Speaking to myself was permissible now I was completely alone and getting used to it. This was no time to check in the mirror for tell-tale lines around my mouth. There was no comfort in bright light and heavy traffic. There was no longer the comfort of turning to John at every juncture for confirmation of a feeling, or some advice about something I already had decided. There was a dawning knowledge it was the case, though, through at least the last five years of our long marriage. I more and more often made things out myself. I knew what I wanted, yet deferred to him out of what – politeness? Reassurance? Companionship? Habit? Too hard to work out. Dubious, random analysis was without question best kept out of the car in complicated Italian traffic. They drove like demons, never batted an eyelid, and terrified the wits out of this driver, used to Australian traffic and drivers in larger cars, who obeyed signs and signals, rules and everything, as a matter of course.

Here, they charged onward, missing each other, and me, by a hairsbreadth, with a margin of seconds, quite happily breaking road rules, but merging like magic, and never interrupting the flow. Yes, magic. I could get used to it. Could I? Could I abandon everything I had in Australia and live in Italy? Among these brinkman drivers? With fine lines around my mouth?

It was a question I had to ask myself, because of the bequest. Also, there was the combination of feelings aroused by John's departure, and all the reawakened memories of a childhood spent more or less in an Italian way.

There were of course a number of bureaucratic hurdles to leap. I still held my UK citizenship, but without a passport. I could possibly obtain the right papers to reside in Italy. The European Union and the Schengen Agreement allowed it, without much difficulty, I was told. The prospect of weeks of form-filling and interviews, though, was not attractive.

I did have weeks. I had as much time I liked. I did not have to be anywhere for anyone. There was no one to share things with either. I could do what I pleased, but would it please me?

Before bureaucracy, I had to address my mental and financial situation. Money, now – since finding the crumpled lotto ticket – was not a real issue. So time, age, desires, plans, energy, and ability; these were the aspects I had to address. Not for me a breakneck dash into a future full of doubt and unknowns, despite a gradual getting used to having cash in the bank. One or two of my siblings would doubtless have raced impulsively towards their fate, if I remembered their personalities well, and if they still acted in the same precipitous, devil-may-care attitudes of their childhood.

It was fortunate my writing could be done anywhere I pleased. A literary career is fully portable. Turning a new page at fifty-eight – or thereabouts – was not something someone like me did without the necessary contemplation of all the pros and cons. Would I still have been this cautious twenty years ago?

My heart was not broken twenty years ago. I had to pull myself up. I drew up abruptly behind a delivery van and thought about *my heart*. Like anybody else, I did have my share of adolescent pangs which seemed like the end of the world as I knew it, when boyfriends came and went. Still, the way a heart is broken at fifty-eight is not the same as when it gets fractured at nineteen.

But where on earth was Via Pietro Mascagni? I found myself going past one orange building for the third time. Going round in circles, I was, slowly; infuriating someone behind me now, who beeped his strident horn and vroomed around my little rental. All right, all right. Ah, there – the inviting and rare opportunity of a vacant diagonal parking space was not to be ignored. Not in Italy. I took it, easily and with some relief.

I found her.

I found her in a little ground floor apartment in a big block of putty-coloured flats with balconies. Not as old or decrepit as I expected.

'It's me. It's Paola, Matilde.'

'*O cielo!* It is you.' She made such a fuss of me. It was so heartening to be welcomed so warmly. I placed a bunch of flowers in her arms, and we crushed it between us in a hearty embrace.

'*Tesorin! Tesoro!*' She called me her treasure, her little treasure, like she always did, and I thought back to the last time I saw her. It could have been some time after my second series was published, I thought. Too long.

The changes were few – although thinner and greyer, she seemed sprightly, and led me to a little sitting room, where a younger woman sat. 'This is my niece, she looks after me, now I need looking after!' She gazed directly at the pale woman in a pink cardigan. 'Say hello to Paola, Anna – she has come to visit and chat. All the way from Australia. Her mother ... ah! Her mother is now with the angels.'

All I could do was nod in agreement and salutation, at once. Matilde took my hand, hooked it under her arm and patted it, like she would do when I was little.

It was a pleasant enough room, and while I was settled into an easy chair, Matilde went to hers, and creaked into an upright position which obviously favoured her back.

'It's been many years, Matilde.'

'Eh? It's like yesterday, my dear. How easily you slip into the old language with me. You were always clever with languages. I don't imagine you can speak much Italian in Australia.'

Someone had said she was very deaf, but she seemed to understand everything I said. 'It all comes back to me.'

'You have a lovely voice. Very clear. Very sharp. Hear this, Anna?' She regarded her niece, who was arranging my flowers in a too-small vase. 'I hear everything she says, everything my Paola says.' She smiled at me, eyes clear and happy. 'Now let me tell you why I was not there on the day ...'

'At the funeral.'

'Yes – you must have wondered. Your mother and I ... ha ha! We prepared ourselves, you see. We made plans. We agreed with one another. So we said our goodbyes in our way, our way. We always agreed about things.'

'Yes, you did.'

'She was lovely. A real lady. A real angel. Given to strange impulses, but lovely, lovely.'

Strange impulses? I did not remember Mama

153

behaving impetuously at all.

'You see, one needs to be impulsive as a woman. One has to do things quickly, when the time and opportunity present themselves. One must be prepared ... to jump! She understood what she wanted to do, and she did it. Her motto was *festina lente*.'

I had an idea what it meant. 'Hasten slowly?'

'You were always a bright girl. Yes. Do you still have your phenomenal memory, eh?'

I had to smile. Phenomenal. 'I remember things, yes. Matilde – you planned with Mama we should all come to see you.'

'Eh? Eh?' She faced me, tilting her head. It meant her hearing was erratic, not always sharp.

I went on. 'I would have come to see you anyway, you know.'

She rotated her head, and I saw why. It was her left ear. I went round to sit on her right, and she wagged a finger at me. 'How quick you are, Tesorin. What a treasure you always were. Promise me ...'

'Yes.'

Matilde gave a high-pitched laugh and slapped palms on knees. 'Wonderful! Wonderful – a sign of real generosity. You say *yes*, not ask *what*.' She beamed again. 'Be careful to whom you give this delightful generosity.'

'Matilde – I'm nearly sixty.'

'You are fifty-eight.'

'It might be a bit too late for it to matter.'

'Never. Never too late. It always matters – down to the last five minutes of your life. Your mother had it. She knew it. Her generosity was the clever kind.'

Anna, the busy niece, brought in a tray laid with an embroidered cloth. And yes – there was a plate of *cantuccini* next to the coffee pot and little cups.

'You still bake.'

'Eh?'

'You still make biscotti – it's wonderful.'

'Ha ha! I knew at thirteen I would die in the kitchen ... some kitchen ... somewhere. Now, drink your coffee, and I'll take you inside – to my bedroom. I have something for you ...' She did not stoop or shuffle, something remarkable at her age. 'And later, we will have some *vin santo* with one of those biscuits. Do you remember how ...?'

I stopped. There was her enormous bed, and propped up against its foot was the painting. Basile's painting. The umbrellas at Santa Maria. 'Matilde!' I whipped around.

Her face was solemn, her eyes bright. 'Look at it, look at it. Beautiful. Your mother wanted you to have it, my love. It is only for you, a bit of a *segreto*, you know.'

I saw why it was a secret. So Mama knew how I felt at sixteen, at seventeen. She guessed about my affection for Basile. I tried to hold back tears, and somehow managed.

'*Bello*, eh?'

'Yes, beautiful.' I leaned forward and peered closely at the picture. The paint had cracked and crazed a little, but it only made it appear more atmospheric, a bit hazy. There was Basile's signature, on a small umbrella on the right, as I instantly remembered. 'I came all the way to Fiesole, knowing it was the only thing I wanted.'

'Take it with you to Australia.'

'To Australia!' It would have been too complicated to tell her I might be making other plans. Besides, they were not fully-formed plans yet. 'Matilde – this is an incredible surprise. Where is ... do you know what happened to Basile?'

'Pick it up and bring it with you. You look like you need some *vin santo!*' She laughed and walked back ahead of me. 'Anna – pour the wine!' Her *ciabatte* clattered on the tiled floor. They were the style of slip-ons she always wore around the house. Very little about her had changed. Her observations were no different. 'So you all coped with the day?'

'Suzanna ... she coped by wearing red shoes.'

'Ha ha!'

'Brod and Nigel needed sympathy from others.'

'And they found some in you, yes?'

'I tried, Matilde, I said a few words to each of them, even Suzanna, but I don't know ... something in me keeps them distant.'

'You are strong, Tesoro. But the strongest sometimes need the most sympathy. Who was there for you, eh? Who?'

She was not trying to comfort me, but to show me something. How could she guess my aloneness? It had to be plain in my face.

'You flew alone from Australia?'

I nodded.

'You do not seek sympathy. It's not pride that separates you from your siblings, you know. Ah ... in English you have no real word for *superbia*, but you know what I mean.'

'You mean hubris?'

'Maybe – you are insulated, like a ... do you remember how Donato used to lag pipes? Insulated, in his way, to prevent things. You protect yourself before you are attacked.'

'Do I?'

'And surprises get you when you are least protected, of course.'

'I know. John has left me, Matilde.'

'Ah! I saw it in your face at the door. You have now ... oh. Oh! There is no mother to comfort you now, *Tesorin*. Come here.' She embraced me, so sweetly it was hard to hold back tears.

'It was such a shock. So sudden.'

'It clears the way, my treasure. It clears the way so you can find contentment. He could not have made his mind up in a day. Nothing is sudden for those who do the leaving. Your mother would have told you this. I tell you in her place.'

I could not say a word.

She let me go and gazed into my face. 'Your mother ...' Matilde crossed herself. 'She would have given you comfort. She would have understood, you know. Bless her dear heart. Your mother might have been impulsive, especially when it came to ... listen – you are old enough now.'

I laughed. 'I might be, Matilde.'

'She said she would never find another love like your father, so it didn't matter one way or another who she had fun with, or with whom she spent a holiday here and there. She was impulsive, not like you, and for an Englishwoman, quite *appassionata*, but ... she and Basile!' She cleared her throat.

I waited for her to pause, make her observations, and continue.

'Basile was not of the same nature, you see. There was not an impetuous bone in his body, that man. Basile, after a while, removed himself from the picture, my dear. You might know why.'

I did remember how deliberate he was. How precise. It was why his portraits were so sought after, but he painted very few. Landscapes and streetscapes were what was he mostly did. I thought, and thought, but could find no reason why he would leave. 'I don't know ...'

'He did not love easily. We all know the type. But when he did, like Donato, he loved deeply, and forever.' She leaned forward, and placed a hand on the small of her back. 'You were very dear to Basile, Paola.' There was a meaningful flicker in her eye. 'And you know you loved him too.'

The hairs on the back of my neck prickled. 'And Mama ...'

'Your Mama was not stupid. She might have been fancy-free and impetuous, but she liked spontaneity, not recklessness. She was a caring and careful mother.'

I didn't know what to say. Emotion gripped me, and would not let go. I only realised my eyes were full of tears when Anna placed a small box of tissues in my lap.

'So after a few summers, when you developed into a most delightful young woman – do you remember wearing your mother's pearls! – after a few years, he disappeared. Not for him such sorts of complication. Not for him. A most moral and upright person. He never married, you know. Never.'

'How do you know?'

'His name! He became quite famous around Naples.'

'He went south.'

She agreed, and indicated I should help myself to a glass from Anna's tray. Her delectable *vin santo*. 'Back to his people. Back to painting the famous bay. A couple of years after he died, there was a brief biography on the television.' She nodded again, and sipped wine. 'Have a *cantuccio* with this. *Perfetto!*'

Out of politeness I nibbled a biscuit and drank some of the wine. She was right, it was perfect. The reaction to hearing of Basile's death, though, made me breathless, and I choked on a biscuit crumb, which made my tearful eyes worse.

'*Tesoro! Carina!* You are moved by the emotion. My dearest Paola, he was an old man, and he left a wealth of paintings of the bay of Naples, of Pompeii, Solfatara, and other places around Campania. He became quite famous. They catalogued his works.'

'There was a programme on television.' Anna wanted to impress, and she did. 'They showed how he was buried underneath a spreading tree, as his very name demanded. *Sottalbero.*'

'What else?' How could I have missed all this, all Basile's life?

They told me as much as they knew. After half an hour, we loaded the painting into the boot of the small car, embraced, and I started the long way back, wondering whether I would ever see Matilde again.

Nigel

Exasperation

Paola returned to find us all arguing on the terrace. I heard her climb the big staircase to her room, and she appeared a minute later in the terrace doorway, looking out to where we all sat. For a moment she cut a silhouette, but when she approached, there was no doubt, from the expression on her face, that she had heard our loud voices.

'How was Matilde?'

Paola emerged onto the darkening terrace. 'It's chilly out here now. Have you been out here the whole time?' She peered from one face to another, her mouth a straight pale line, her eyes sharp. Her expression no longer felt like she wanted to stick something sharp in each of our eyes. 'What's ... what are you discussing?' Her voice was not as composed as her face.

'Are we being loud? Did you hear us ...?'

'I could hear you from the car.'

'Arguing! About the will. Whether or not to accept it!' Suzanna's voice seemed a touch too soft, intentionally lowered, for effect. In the gathering dusk, she seemed ruffled, with pink cheeks and visible teeth; an angered cat.

I stood back and watched the three of them. Suzanna fidgety and fretful, Brod apparently guilty he had introduced the topic, even though he knew it would have to be mentioned at some point, and newly-arrived Paola perplexed and tired by her drive to Prato, struggling to stay calm. No, pacified by something. Her visit with Matilde must have made a difference.

'Let me pour you a drink.' I tried not to sound like a peacemaker, but it was precisely how it came out.

At last Paola answered my question. 'Matilde is in excellent health and spirits. It was such a lovely visit. She's well cared for by her niece. Quite easy to find, too – if you know where to start!' She sat and sighed. 'I'll give you all directions – I wish I'd had some myself.' She realized she had sliced our argument in half, and appeared like she had no desire for it to resume, even though it was she who wanted to discuss the will all along.

'I'll have to continue dinner soon,' I said, further fracturing the momentum of the lively discussion.

'I thought we were going out.' Suzanna had settled somewhat.

'And I thought we were all of one mind about accepting Mama's will. There's the important *documento* to sign.' Brod stared at Paola.

Harriet placed a hand over her forehead in exasperation. 'Brod – it was you who raised the question. It was you.'

'And I was speaking to Nigel ...' He seemed to resent Harriet's participation.

'Oh!'

I remembered it was when Grant had quietly left the terrace earlier, leaving us to what was obviously a private family conference. I wondered if the others minded my wife taking such an active part in it, since even Lewis was invisible, heavy navy sweater zipped up to his chin, blurring into the darkening sky, happy to listen without saying a word.

Brod smiled and fairly bisected his face from ear to ear. In the deepening gloom, with the dusky indigo sky a backdrop emphasizing the size of his ears, he was comical. The moustache was awful. I had an idea he might have teased us all into a state of fury and doubt, quite on purpose.

He opened both palms and waggled long fingers. 'It was a mere hypothetical. I asked what might happen if we didn't all accept the will. What if one of us didn't think it was equitable ... and I didn't specify who ... it could be any of us.'

Suzanna bridled. 'And here I was thinking you were about to upset the applecart!' Her own wide mouth smiled at her twin, but her eyes blazed, even in the half-darkness. 'You were always one to make trouble when there was none.'

'What!' Brod burst into sarcastic laughter. 'What?'

I quickly stood and started to say something. 'And I think ...'

'You think you can pour Fiesole olive oil over troubled waters, Nige. I think we'd all better have a jolly good shouting match and get it over with.' Harriet sat back, obviously fed up.

Paola's eyes travelled from one pair of eyes to another in turn, bemused and mute. She seemed to have no doubt about anything at all. Her visit to Matilde had done something to soothe her, in her aloneness. 'Let's all go down to some bistro ...'

'The nice *osteria* ...'

'Oh, please, not where all the tourists gather, Brod.'

I put a hand up. 'Let's not fight about this too.'

Harriet stood. 'If we want to avoid the tourists and have a nice meal at a long table ... are Lori and Tad coming? ... in which case we should go to the place whose name I can never remember. The one with all the bikes hanging from the ceiling.'

'Oh, yes.'

'Wonderful.'

'Okay – lead the way!'

'Can we walk?'

'Is it far away?'

'Won't Paola be tired after her drive?'

It was clear we all wanted to clear the air. The mound of chopped vegetables could always be blanched and frozen.

My older sister regarded me boldly and without guile. When everyone had left the terrace, she hung back.

I stood with my back to the cobalt sky, where a threatening bank of cloud had gathered, feeling a chill breeze blowing past me from over Florence. The trees had all turned black. It was until then a beautiful clear night, but would grow quite cold later. 'What is it, Paola?'

'I'm very happy with how Mama apportioned the bequests. Aren't you, Nigel? We ... we all sat there, that afternoon, listening to the notary, hardly exchanging glances, all hoping it wouldn't cause too much complicated calculation, division, signatures, powers of attorney, acting as joint vendors, buying each other out of things ...' She took a deep breath and took up one of the chairs to take inside. 'I was afraid Italian bureaucracy and the funny succession laws they have here would make it all impossible to decipher and execute. He read it so it all sounded simple. Or is it too good to be true? Aren't you happy with how Mama devised it all, Nigel?'

I picked up two chairs from their backs and started toward the sitting room door. 'Of course I am. I'm delighted.'

'I could see it in your face.'

Could she really? I tilted my head in question. Ah – my sister Paola. She had a habit of examining people silently, and it could be quite unnerving. 'I thought Mama was very clever. I think it's all perfect.'

'And do you know what I think? I think Brod is stirring.'

I had to agree. 'What he said last. A hypothetical, he said.'

'Could it be he's not happy, Nigel?'

I stopped to think on the threshold of the glass door to the terrace. Yellow light from the sitting room spilled out in a long rectangle onto the terrace floor. A curtain moved in the breeze. From somewhere in the valley, the sounds of a brass band were clearly audible. We listened together. American fanfare music; Sousa, as far as I could guess, in Tuscany.

I had to say something. 'Brod can be strange, and he can fluff up all our feathers. He could have no reason to be unhappy with his portion.'

Paola shook her head. 'No, no – I mean unhappy for some other reason. Something to do with his new relationship.'

'But ...' I thought it over for a second. 'They seem quite all right. Grant is a very nice chap. The only thing Brod should do is shave off his silly moustache.'

She shifted in the light from the sitting room, lifted the chair through, and walked along to the kitchen. She set down the chair, and faced me. 'You can have two perfectly nice people, in a relationship with some very prickly problems. No one's going to come out with their private stuff at a reunion like this. Things do surface, though, don't they, despite all efforts to present a face. Behaviour and words ... they betray everyone's feelings and moods. Besides – we're all here because Mama died.' She looked at her feet. 'It's difficult to introduce more ... more personal matters.'

So she knew something about Grant and Brod. I wasn't about to ask. 'More personal ... like you and John.'

Her eyes were clear when her face rose to mine. She pushed at a lock of hair, which the breeze had blown into her face, with a steady hand. 'I'm getting used to it. I'll be fine. I'm going to be all right, Nigel. But no – you're right. I'm not about to bring it up as a big discussion for all and sundry to tear apart and analyse.'

'No.' I agreed with her. 'No one likes to have their marriage dissected at a dining room table, after the main course, before dessert.'

She laughed. It was good to hear her laugh in such an unusually hearty way. Something happened at Matilde's, and it had lightened her heart.

Suzanna

Needless stirring and teasing

I knew what Brod was stewing about. Of course I knew. A twin's thoughts are never entirely secret. He was brooding about his relationship with Mama. Was her love for him faithfully and unerringly equal to hers for me? What a dilemma to have, when one is half of something! Although I suspected siblings all had a craving for special regard from a parent, the preoccupation was worse for twins!

We had only one parent for the portion of our childhood we could remember. For the part that most probably truly mattered. We all, except Paola, had very fragile memories of Papa, and they were memories created out of narrative and family folklore, rather than authentic recollections. We were all second-hand witnesses to what he did and who he was. All dead parents were saints. Mama was turning into one right now, under all our noses.

Paola of course had what she termed the curse of a long memory. She might have remembered some of Papa's faults and errors. Or may have realized sainthood was not something one could confer on our mother. Was there such a thing as a parent who entirely lacked flaws and weaknesses? I for one remembered Mama singling out my older sister when it came to selecting clothes for the winter. She spent much more time with her than with me. Or with the boys.

I was infuriated by Brod's teasing and stirring out on the terrace, and Paola was not there to rein him in with a clearly rational observation based on some real memory, or some logical calculation. She appeared late, unusually relaxed, and unwilling to enter an argument started without her. She missed her calling – Paola should have gone into the law. What a formidable unflappable judge she would have made!

What a transparent thing for Brod to do! Stirring us all up about the bequest. Transparent at least to me. I thought he was quite happy with it all, and that he would sign the d*ichiarazione di successione* without a murmur. It appeared, however, that Nigel, who had most at stake apparently, and who desperately needed us all to sign, was ruffled and upset. Nigel was the most likely to sign without much hesitation, and my guess was Paola had no reason not to.

I was rather elated with my portion of the estate. For two reasons; the most important one being I would not have to surrender, sell, or buy out any one of my siblings. I was singled out quite amazingly cleverly by Mama. Oh, Mama! Clever, without being scheming. Intelligent and fair, but infinitely understanding of me in particular. Perhaps I would have to live it down with the others.

How dreadful being the female half of a pair of twins might have been with a chauvinistic parent, or one driven by popular beliefs, and prejudices, and social preferences! At least Mama saw the hazards late in life, even though I had to fight for attention too often when I was young.

My second reason was of course the boat. I had planned, schemed and worked all my life with an aim in mind. Papa taught us all to work towards aims. Or so Mama used to tell us, all the summer long. Mine was to sail the Med. Persuading Lewis took a long time, but I guessed he would relent because all he wanted was for us to be comfortable together. Comfort for Lewis was not a simple thing. It had to be physical and mental. He was a complex man. I realized he seemed to everyone to be a dogsbody, a yes-man, an auxiliary, a side-kick to my activities and ventures, but he has been no small help. He is a collaborator of very fine quality, who can strategize and implement plans, working flexibility into financial policies and logistical procedures without which I would have floundered a long time ago. No one can buy and sell franchises on their own. Lewis is like the scullery of this house, the old scullery which holds up the entire building, it and its formidable buttresses.

He made me realize, very early in our relationship, the likelihood was I would not make a great parent. We debated what it would mean to have a family, and I had to agree I wanted my plans and dreams to materialize much more than I wanted to be a mother. He was happy with the decision.

'I'm a private person who would not cope well with sticky interruptions, sleepless nights, and four-hourly feeds, Suzanna. You are pretty much the same,' he said. It was only years later I realized he was clearing the way for a future he could handle. 'The fact we are discussing this at all is a good indicator, darling – and it's why I brought it up.'

It was years before I realized what he meant. He was also right about his feelings about the will.

I could have laughed out loud in surprise when we all sat so solemnly in Mama's sitting room with the notary. Did they all see me raise a hand to cover an involuntary smile? Mama set me free of my siblings. She insulated me, made me feel special, in the same way as she would single me out as a child, very early on a Saturday morning, when she'd tap a knuckle on my door, put her head into the room, and hiss, 'Suzanna ... I made us pancakes!' No one else heard. We'd sit in the big warm kitchen and stuff ourselves with blackberry pancakes, oozing with dark juice.

'Eat them while they're warm ... here's more sugar.'

She sensed how being a younger sister, how being a twin, how being a young woman, was not the easiest thing. She gave me strength and distinction.

'You'll go far, my darling,' she would say, tapping her garden-stressed fingers on the red table top. 'Very much your own little person. You are a determined young thing.'

And we'd talk about school, about friends, about my agony over the right haircut and the visibility of steel braces on my awful teeth! She made time feel like a stretchable or shrinkable commodity. I learned so much from Mama's concept of time and how to get it to work for me.

'Do you know what Papa used to say, Suzanna?' She asked me this one Saturday morning when the sun sizzled early outside and she felt it would be a dreadfully humid day. I was all ears, all replete after eating half a dozen pancakes and drinking a bowl of warm milk to which she had added a splash of coffee from the intractable filter machine. 'Papa said everything was either time or money. Now you, of all people, would understand the ... the concept.'

And I kept the concept in mind my entire career. Everything in business, indeed, was time or money! But Mama gave me a gardening example, which stayed in my head, more than Papa's behest ever could. 'You can plant a sapling and wait for five years for a good crop of fruit ... which is time. Or you can buy an advanced, more expensive, tree and have fruit the same year. That's money.'

So I always measured cost against waiting, in business. And found someone like Lewis who always estimated what he called my acumen above his own. Only a generous and very clever man without an inflated ego could do what Lewis did. I've been so lucky!

Brod

A sweet grannie

I insisted on Grant driving with me to Matilde's, all the way to Prato. We followed Paola's directions and got there rather quickly, despite the gridlock traffic we encountered as we entered town. There was the tall orange building she mentioned, and yes, a mushroom-coloured apartment block, where Matilde and her niece lived.

'O, *guarda, guarda!*' She was so delighted to see me, clapping her hands like a child and beaming, beaming – she took both my hands in hers, as she would when I was little, but she was gratefully too short now to sweep my hair backwards off my forehead.

She shook Grant's hand and tried her English on him, which seemed hilarious to her too, so we all stood in her narrow hallway and hooted with laughter. It was good.

Grant gave me a little shake of his head,

followed by a quick nod and wink, which meant I didn't have to constantly translate back and forth. He was happy to sit there and watch me converse with Matilde, who told me all about how Donato spent his last year, and how he had carved a massive owl out of a tree stump, slowly chiselling and whittling over the twelve months he was poorly; unwilling to sit and do nothing.

'He did not wait to die, he worked right to the end, filling the room with sawdust and shavings, and laughing when I tried to sweep and dust. Come, I'll show you!' She led up a passage to a small spotless bedroom, where a beautiful fruitwood owl stood on a chest. '*M'ha lasciato un gufo!*' She laughed, but there was a slight tremor in her voice and she impatiently brushed a tear from her cheek. 'He left me an owl, an owl, a preying bird that flies at night, and I cannot find a reason why. I think for once he wanted to do something without reason.'

'Did he ...?'

'Never, never. Everything he did had a reason, like when he planted those new pine trees in a row, to please your mother. Goodness knows how tall they must be now. Close to the house. Close. Sheltering. The owl? No reason.'

I think she did see some sort of reason, and I was quite touched to see her emotion. She sat us in her small kitchen and gave us some sweet yellowish wine and her famous almond biscuits.

Grant held up his glass. 'Mm – what is this? It's delicious.'

'Trebbiano grapes,' she said. 'Explain to your friend, Broderick. This is Tuscan *vin santo*, and look

– the colour is gold.' She held up her small stemmed glass and light from the kitchen window lit it up, amber.

She explained about her relatives, who had a vineyard somewhere in the hills on the other side of Florence. Her niece Anna bowed her head, poured us all a little more wine, and peeped at something baking in the wall oven.

'More biscuits, more *cantuccini*. I often send a little basket of them to the nuns at the *monastero* di San Clemente. There are still nuns there, you know. They live *in clausura* ... how do you ...?'

'Cloistered – isolated from the world, am I right?'

She agreed. 'They rely on the community to keep food on their table, you know. They are Dominicans. It is a very old monastery. Very old, medieval,' she went on, in her Florentine dialect, which was clear and easy to follow. 'There are still a few nuns there, shut away from the world. They hardly speak to each other. A life of prayer and contemplation.' She smiled and cocked an eye at me. 'I suppose there need to be some nice pious people to make up for the rest of us, wicked as we are.' She chuckled.

'Wicked?'

'Eh?'

I could see her hearing came and went. Her face was tired. 'We can't stay long, Matilde.'

She had turned her good ear to me and tilted her head. 'But not before we speak a bit about your dear mother – what a wonderful woman she was, eh? And how clever in the garden. Ah, la signora Nina!'

'She outlived Papa ...'

'... by quite a few years, yes. So she made sure you four children knew him, by talking about him and what he did. All those rooms he renovated at the villa!'

'Mm – the villa needs a lot of repairs now.'

'My advice?' Her shrewd eyes opened wide, as wide as the deep wrinkles and papery eyelids allowed. 'You should keep it. One of you. Some of you. All of you? There should be a *signore* or *signora* Larkin at the villa forever! Keep it, have a couple of men like Pierino, who is Anna's brother here, do some work. He is a good handyman. It's all you need. Slowly, slowly – it's how you should do it. Isn't it so, Anna?'

Her niece made a motion of assent. She sat in a corner of the room, away from the table, with her arms folded comfortably over her rounded stomach, chewing a biscuit. 'Pierino is very good. He will be more than happy to work at the villa.'

Grant had no notion of what the conversation was about. He sipped his wine and glanced at me, at Matilde, and on to Anna, and back to me. We would have to go soon, or he would be bored rigid.

'We'll go soon, Grant.'

'No – this visit is important. Isn't it? Don't worry about me. It's not like it happens every weekend, Brod.' He waved an emphatic hand and I could see he wished he had such people to visit, in Italy, or anywhere.

'Now listen, before you go, I must tell you a secret only you will hear. Are you listening?'

'Yes, Matilde.'

'Eh?'

'I'm listening.'

'There was something your mother wanted you to have, Brod-er-ick.'

It was so funny, so reminiscent of my childhood, to have her call me by my full name. I remembered her scolding me for running over a tiled floor she had mopped. *Brod-er-ick!* I reminded her of how she would shake the mop at me.

'Ha ha! You were such a naughty boy. You used to steal things from your big sister's room, and I occasionally used to take books and comics from under your bed, and put them back in the box under hers! Ha ha!'

We all laughed again, Grant not knowing what amused us so heartily, his eyes gazing from one face to another, and enjoying it anyway.

'Listen, *carino*, listen. Go and search up in the roof of the back house. You know very well – the back house where Donato and I used to live? Go to the little house, and up in the roof space, in the ... what do you call it?'

'The attic?'

'Ecco – *il sottotetto*. Yes – up in the attic you will find something your beautiful mother wanted you to have, only you. Don't tell anyone else, *capito?*'

I understood. 'But what is it, Matilde?'

She smiled in a mysterious way. 'It will be very clear when you find it. *Buona fortuna, caro.*'

She wished me good fortune, in exactly the same way as she would when we all went back to school in the autumn, when we were kids. I could see she was tired. I kissed her on both cheeks and Grant and I made our farewells and walked back to the car.

'Such a sweet little grannie, she is.'

'Oh Grant – she used to have such energy. She practically ran the villa ... chasing us, cooking, cleaning, ironing, keeping Mama company in the garden from time to time. It couldn't have been easy, with four kids making such a noise and such a mess.'

'And talking, talking, talking!'

I twisted sideways. 'Do we talk a lot?'

Grant laughed. 'Do you talk! And you all have the same habit of saying something three times, in three different ... distinct ... varied ... ways!' He held up three fingers as he said the words.

'Mama's speech patterns were ... well, repetitive. Are mine?'

'You all do it.'

'Matilde became used to us and our mess and noise ... and repetition ... I suppose.'

'She treasured every minute, if her eyes reflected anything.'

'I guess so. What do you think is in the attic at the small back house, up at the villa, then?'

'What attic? You've got to tell me what went on. I couldn't understand a word, the way you gabbled on and on!'

I laughed and explained what Matilde had said about something hidden in the attic, as we drove all the way back to Fiesole.

'Do you think she actually meant I should keep it a secret?'

'If it's a bag of gold coins you feasibly could, but if it's anything bigger you'd have to explain to the other three.'

'Hm. I'll have a peep before we all leave tomorrow.'

'I'm looking forward to coming back, Brod.'

'Ha ha, Grant. We'll have to make real decisions about all that at some point. We must still have the big final deciding discussion.'

I gazed out of the car window and wondered what we would end up doing, about the villa, about the inheritance, about the way it had all gone. I didn't know whether to be grateful to Mama for how she had divided it all up; or to be sorry I stirred such an argument up the night before, and infuriated Suzanna. I also seemed to have scared Nigel. Poor Nigel – I didn't mean to jolt him. It's gone absolutely the right way for him.

There was still the question of Paola. Although a bit less wound up than the day we all arrived, and a bit less nervous than on the day of the funeral, my older sister seemed sometimes edgy and sometimes composed; exerting enormous control over her emotions and every word she let out of her mouth. Surely she wasn't always so? I should get her alone and have a nice long chat. I had nearly forgotten her long marriage had only recently broken down and I still hadn't said a word to her about it all.

I might corner her in the hall, in front of the wall gods, in front of her Neptune, and my Diana and her fading hounds, quite as I used to do as a boy, and sweeten her up with something like roller skates or a box of books or ... I wonder how she would react if I mentioned a pallet of young plants?

Paola

Observation

What better place to address a family than at a dinner table in a neutral place, such as a restaurant? We dithered a bit when taking our places, and although I felt I should sit next to Brod, found Grant was somehow inserted between us, with Lori and a reluctant Tad sitting directly across from us.

We all craned our necks up to the bikes swinging above us, in the updrafts of breath, laughter, and the aromas of food from plated dinners coming out of the kitchen.

'Let's talk about the *dichiarazione di successione.*' It was obviously easier to use those words than the English equivalent.

They all stopped talking and looked at me. Did I seem ready to them, to discuss what had been on all our minds since we sat in Mama's sitting room in front of the pompous notary, Dottor Umberto Ugobaldi, in his steel-rimmed specs?

No one disagreed, but there was not a word

179

from our table for a long interlude, and chatter came in from others. The clink-chink-dingle of crockery, cutlery, and glassware was all about us.

'Before we do,' Suzanna said, raising her head and glass and demanding attention, 'I should say I'm going to see Matilde tomorrow. Lewis and I ought to be on our way very soon. That boat won't wait for us forever. We can make an offer right now. A good one.'

'Oh? So you're not buying it new?'

I sighed at Brod's question and glared at him. Did he not know some boats were special, and that our sister could talk forever about it? It would stretch Suzanna's side-bar and take more time than I had patience for. I wanted to talk about Mama's bequest and how – or whether – it would affect the ways we were starting to think about things. Was everyone willing to sign the acceptance document? I wanted to know, and was pretty certain we all did. If everyone was leaving soon, we'd have to sign quickly.

My sister smiled. 'Lewis and I have found the ideal sailing boat – it has a history. It's the very same vessel Alex de Cassius took around the world!' A bit dismayed at the blank faces, she went on. 'Alex de Cassius took *Char-à-banc* around the world last year, after his umpteenth Sydney-Hobart race, in which he's never come in later than tenth! Surely ... oh, all right, you don't know!' She laughed and looked around at us all once more.

'So it's a famous boat, Suzanna?' I had to say something to hurry the topic along.

'Yes, very famous, and we are texting and emailing away, right now, with Alex, to tell him we're very interested.'

'What kind is it?' Brod in all probability knew less than I did about boats. Perhaps he was truly curious.

Suzanna's eyes brightened, as Harriet's glazed over. My sister smiled. 'A Kaufman Forty-Seven, a cutter, it is. Lots of room, and we can have crew – two, or three, put up in the aft cabin.'

'Crew!'

Lori's eyes widened. 'Wow – three Popeyes in blue and white.'

We all laughed.

'So how big ...'

'Nearly sixteen metres ... in length.'

I was surprised at its size. It sounded like a very expensive craft. 'Where's the boat right now?'

'Malta. *Char-à-banc* is in Malta, which is quite convenient, you'll agree, so I'll hop on a plane as soon as possible, Lewis will take Otto home to be cared for, won't you, darling? And by the end of the month she'll be on a hard stand being de-fouled, re-rigged and all, ready for us to take her to ... ' She counted off on long fingers. '... Piraeus, Venice, Portofino, Lisbon, Istanbul, Villefranche-sur-Mer, ... and much later on to Cowes. It's so exciting.' She shook her head at the immobile little pet whose snout rested on her forearm. The dog had hardly moved since their arrival in Fiesole. I doubt I had heard the tiniest yelp, whine, or growl.

'Will the dog ... um, will Otto go with you on the boat at some stage?'

Her eyes widened. 'Of course. Eventually – he needs his proper shots and things soon. There's forty-seven feet of boat. Plenty of room for Otto!'

'All settled and decided, you sound, Suzanna.' Nigel sat at the end with Harriet on his right. They both nodded in the same way.

'Very nearly settled. There's one other very interested party, but we should be able to put in a solid decent bid now. *Char-à-banc* is very nearly ours!'

'It's an unusual name for a boat.' I might as well carry on with the conversation. There would be time enough to discuss the will. I was starting to doubt whether we would ever hear each other's opinions on signing the document. I poured more wine and sat back, prepared to listen to Suzanna.

Unusually for him, Lewis replied, after carefully placing his fork on an empty plate. 'It's a French word meaning a carriage with wooden benches. Or an early type of open bus. Amusing. Amusing name for a boat, but it's obvious why it was given such a name.'

I could hear Brod hum from where I sat. 'No, it isn't, Lewis. Why's it obvious?'

'Well, Brod – the de Cassius family had one of the most famous bus companies in France and Italy ... you know, along the Riviera, for decades. Nearly a hundred years. There's still a trucking company called de Cassius somewhere.'

'In Belgium. They have a picture of our boat on the office wall!' Suzanna seemed very confident they would bring off the purchase.

'The very same one!'

'Yes, we've seen it on the internet. So we're very keen, aren't we, Lewis?'

Lewis seemed like he had to work on *keen*, but was not far from happy. Making Suzanna happy was what he was all about.

'Well.' Now I could divert them all to talk about the will. No, not yet. Someone ordered more wine, and we were all talking about desserts and coffees. 'Well – so Mama's foresight has set you up fantastically well, Suzanna.'

What could she do but nod and smile? 'Yes, of course. I didn't know it was what she was going to do. I thought she would leave a … you know, what people would term a normal will, in which everything was lumped together and split four ways.'

Nigel lifted his coffee cup. 'Mama was not *people*. There was nothing normal about her. Well, you know what I mean.'

Harriet, who sat so close to her husband their shoulders touched, glanced up from her plate of artfully arranged ice cream. 'She wasn't weird, though. She was extraordinary enough to be unusual … but she wasn't weird.'

I shot her a half scowl which I had no doubt would be seen as disapproving by everyone there. It had reached a point where everyone knew – definitely, after all these years – that Harriet and I would never get on. She tolerated my presence when it was necessary, and no more. Too late, I softened my gaze, when she had looked away.

Despite Harriet's very annoying remark, it developed swiftly into a reminiscent discussion about Mama. Quite comforting. Despite confusing and conflicting memories, we all remembered her well.

183

I planned to forget about the will and enjoy it. The temptation to startle them with memories I thought were unique to my mind had softened a bit, and I resisted the urge to remind them about the time she tried to tackle a fallen tree with a little hacksaw, or how she dealt with one enormous failed canvas, a very big portrait of us all together, which she had stuck into a bonfire between the lawn on the lower terrace and the rubble wall. She had tried to paint us in a group, one summer, and with one thing and another, it became an oddly-planned portrait in colours she thought were 'wrong, all wrong'. She hacked at it in frustration, and we all ended up toasting bits of bread on long sticks around its flames.

'She taught us quite a lot,' Brod said, mostly to Grant.

'She even taught us to do things she couldn't do. Like roller skate.'

I thought about it. 'Oh – true. I never saw her skate. I never saw her dive off the springboard down at the Florence pool, either. But I seem to remember she showed me how.'

'Indeed! Mama taught us how!'

'And she never signed notes or letters with Mama.'

'She got the habit from Papa.' Suzanna leaned forward. 'I still have a birthday card he sent when Brod and I were very little. I think it was my first year at boarding school. It's signed Roland.'

'I got one too.'

'I must have a couple.'

'We all had letters from Mama, two a term. She

never missed one.'

'All signed Nina.'

I risked taking the prompt. 'She signed the will Nina.'

'Paola – this is neither the time, nor the place.' Nigel seemed annoyed.

My gasp reached his ears across the space separating us. 'You didn't want to talk about the will at home, either.'

'Oh, I don't know about you, Paola – but it no longer feels like home to me.' Suzanna made a face.

'Suzanna ... don't.' Even Brod saw how critical her remarks could be.

'No – true. It's either because there are so many of us staying, this time ... '

'We're not staying there.' Brod was quick to put her right.

' ... or because it's fallen into disrepair.'

'It's not so bad.'

'Yes, it is, Nigel, starting with the frescoes in the hall. I don't know why you didn't have them painted over when you and Harriet were caring for Mama. I don't know how you could stand to pass them in and out of the hall ... up and down the stairs ... back and forth to the ...'

Nigel cut Suzanna off. 'We couldn't make such decisions when Mama was still alive!'

Brod leaned toward Grant. 'Grant loves those frescoes.'

His partner gave a slight nod, but I could see his reluctance to enter an animated debate with Suzanna. 'Um - they're quite fabulous, and should be restored. The whole house ...' He paused, and I saw why. Grant did not feel he ought to make any sort of comment, and left it for Brod and his family to discuss. He caught my eye, and I saw a glint of something there. So tactful, so understanding. He was a sensitive man. The world would be an amazing place if more men were like Grant.

'It unquestionably feels like home to me. I mean – we haven't even slept in it, and it feels like home. We should have one night there, eh, Grant?' Brod folded his napkin, finished his coffee, and smiled his broad smile. 'Hm – tomorrow night? Before we drive to the airport?'

'You should.' There was Harriet, using her proprietary tone again. Even after understanding the contents of Mama's will, she still acted like the villa was hers.

I edged forward. 'Yes, Brod, you should.' I addressed his partner. 'You should get a feel for what it's like to wake there, Grant. The morning light. The morning lull, and then the afternoon breeze.'

Harriet seemed a bit stung and withdrew. She grimaced comically at Nigel, who smiled back at her. *It's all right*, he seemed to signal, with a similarly, comically, stretched mouth.

One thing was certain in my mind. Mama knew Harriet and I would never agree on anything, so she had left a carefully thought-out will for a reason. That reason.

Everyone stopped talking when Tad uttered a long clear sentence none of us expected. He was thin, pale, and bit his nails down to the quick, but his voice was surprisingly mature, with a startling tenor register, coming across from me, where he was in the process of demolishing an enormous dessert.

My nephew sounded very adult. 'Gramma's will is a very clever piece of writing. It was as if she was there, telling everyone what the best solution was to everything. Not simply money and houses and necklaces and who should have what. But, you know, about life and love and how everyone ought to go about enjoying stuff.'

His mother gave him a strange glance. His father's jaw dropped. I smiled, rather glad to have someone else declare what we all should have realized earlier. Not even recalling whether he was in the room for the reading, I saw it as a moving statement. I thought his mother might take an example from the way he spoke; rarely, but with infinite meaning.

Lori looked sideways at her brother, amazed he had uttered so many words at once. 'What – like you enjoy your blazer, Tad?'

He regarded his half-finished *crème brûlée*.

'Brod – stay in Basile's room.' I felt they would like that room best, since Brod's old bedroom was so small.

'Basile's room?' Many voices rose at once.

What did I hear in the various tones rising and falling around the table? It was so obvious I was the only one to give any thought to how significant the artist's presence was in all our lives. How easily they forgot. 'Yes – it was Basile's room, for about four summers. He kept his painting gear in the next room. It's the bedroom with rust-coloured walls and the curly cornices. Does no one remember? I remember him painting in there when it was windy.

187

There were canvases stacked along the walls. I remember his bedroom door was always closed.'

'What else?' Grant was always interested when I mentioned art and architectural details. 'I think I've seen the room. The cornices are art nouveau ... sort of.'

'It was one of the rooms Papa renovated, years back. Donato found the taps in the bathroom from some salvage place in Prato.'

'The stuff you remember, Paola.'

'She brings back things I'd never have thought of otherwise.'

'Why do you think you remember so much, Auntie Paola?'

I spoke to Lori. 'I tended to be quiet. I observed a lot.' I laughed. 'A typical oldest-child habit, I guess.'

'One thing I certainly wasn't ... observant. Or quiet!' Suzanna spoke to Lewis, but we all heard, and laughed. You had to give it to Suzanna; she knew herself, and could be unapologetic and funny with it, no matter how acerbically she phrased her words.

Lively conversation started around the table, and the two brothers walked off together to settle the bill. I let them. My head and heart were taken by memories of Basile, who would take and guide my hand with the brush, to trace outlines of some landscape. 'Distance ... remember distance. It's as important between a tree, a hill, and a church as it is between the nose, the lips, and the chin. Distance. Always. Accurate distance means accurate likeness.'

I never painted seriously, and I wondered whether his advice had anything to do with the way I wrote – with my writing style, in which I placed distance between characters, between events, between the premises on which I constructed my stories. Distance between me and my readers? Perhaps there was a bit of Basile in what I did and how I wrote.

Not even I – not even I and my elephantine memory – remembered everything. Matilde had brought some things back to me with such power when everything in my life seemed worthless and confused, now John was no longer in it and I was drifting. After the drive back to Fiesole, I found it was all suddenly clear and full of soothing meaning and direction.

Dinner at the *osteria* was a definite failure. We all returned more distant and close to hostile with each other. Still, I was soothed by recollections brought on by renewing my connection to Matilde. The way she spoke about Basile reawakened the way I felt about him as a teenager. The young woman I no longer was.

Basile had stood there, one day, between the doors leading to his room and the one where all his canvases were stacked; tall, with riveting light-coloured eyes which seemed incredibly sad. How could a sixteen year-old even conceive of adult sadness? How could a young girl, in a checked blue skirt and yellow blouse, with hair pulled back with black velvet ribbon, conceive of what was happening? I could not have been anywhere near guessing how he felt – or even whether there was anything to guess.

He stood there and put his hand lightly on my shoulder. 'In English ... in English, is there only one word for distance? Tell me, Paola, how you say it in English.'

How could I have known what he meant? I thought he meant the distance between a nose and a lip, a lip and a chin. I thought he meant the distance between a tree and a church steeple. 'Distance ...' I said. The woman nearing sixty now saw meaning hidden from the girl of sixteen.

'In Italian, we have *distanza* ... and there is also *lontananza*.'

'Oh.'

'The first ... it is ... it is mechanical, scientific, mathematical. Yes?'

'Yes.'

'For artists, and tailors, and builders, yes?'

'Yes?'

'*La lontananza* is emotional, my sweet.' He made a wry expression. 'It's distance between people. There is a song, by Domenico Modugno. One day you will listen to it ...'

Because it was hard to understand what he meant, all I could do was smile. At sixteen, it felt like sentimentality reserved for adults. At fifty-eight it rang with recognition and regret.

Matilde hinted at his reason for leaving Fiesole. I never saw him again, he put distance between us, because he was – she said – an upright and moral man. He created *lontananza* between us, to protect me, one might think, from what could turn into an inappropriate love.

It would have taken a less cynical woman than myself, at the moment, to consider what might have happened had he been less upright and moral.

The ensuing years were a jumble of recollected flashes of shifts and changes. How I started writing. How I met John. How I ended up, because of and despite some decisions, living in Australia. Years went by without a thought of Basile.

I had his painting. Matilde made sure I did. I knew for a long time it was vital to find it, but I didn't know exactly why. The awakening of a memory, prompted by a departing husband, and an old woman in a tiny apartment in Italy, could seed the desire to own the painting. I truly formed the wish to search for it while sitting in an uncomfortable claustrophobic aeroplane seat all the way from Melbourne, trying to remember a time I felt loved. I had it now; I knew I was well-loved, and the painting was mine. Was it enough?

Nigel

Packing

Paola kept insisting we talk about the will, and the last thing Harriet thought we should do was discuss whether we were all going to sign the acceptance. Of course we were; it was patently obvious none of us had any real reason not to. It would mean personal and financial disaster to me if someone didn't. I hardly had patience to wait another day.

Harriet too seemed stressed. 'Remember what the notary said.'

'Dottor Ugobaldi said a lot of things, Harriet – which of them do you mean?'

'He said acceptance is irrevocable.'

I held out my hands, palms up. I pushed sliding spectacles up my nose again. 'What possible reason could there be to want to revoke?'

'We can't – it's the law. Once a will is accepted, there's no going back.'

'Yes. He was clear about it. Mama left no debts,

no complexities, no knots to untie ... nothing we would ever regret. So ...'

Unless it was to spite each other, no one would renounce; and the time for spite was long past. We might have done it as young people, but not now.

On the way to the room Harriet and I were using, at the end of the wing, I heard music. It was a tinny high-pitched sound, and it came from Paola's room. She was playing something on her laptop. Once more, she was being quiet, scrutinizing our movements and faces and words like a predatory bird before retreating to her nest. Paola was an owl.

The music stopped as I passed, and started again. The same song, some old Italian song from so long ago I could not – would not – dredge my memory for it. Paola was the memory freak, not I, and here she was, playing something that would either replenish, or stimulate, or stop – hopefully – one of her vivid memories. She was right – it was a curse. If I had a similar mental facility, it would have driven me mad.

Harriet had our belongings spread all over the place.

'Packing already?'

'Well, we are leaving tomorrow, darling. We have to leave at some point.' Her voice sounded funny.

'Harriet!'

She stood, shifted slightly, and dropped into my arms. Not quite sobbing, but choked with emotion.

'Are those tears?'

'We lived here long enough, Nige.'

I took a deep breath. 'Harriet. Don't tell me you wanted the house. Oh, sweetheart. You're disappointed we didn't get this house.'

She mumbled something against my chest.

'This is the only clean shirt I have left, darling. What's wrong?'

She laughed. 'Oh, Nigel. We are such stupid, stupid people.'

Whatever made her say such a thing?

'Through the whole afternoon, Nige – through the funeral, through the reading of the will, I kept hoping, hoping, hoping we wouldn't have to give up this house. Part of our lives happened here, and yours ... mostly yours ... since you were a tiny child!' Her voice rose, and it sounded angry. 'Why aren't you upset?'

'Well – now you're getting angry at me!'

'I am!'

I still couldn't understand. Of all siblings, I was the one who came out best. Mama had devised it all perfectly. So a crumbling house in the middle of Fiesole, where everything was so expensive to fix, was gratefully not part of it. I was surprised the others seemed so likely to sign. 'Harriet – look at me. This place will cost an arm and a leg to renovate ... to restore. Some parts need rebuilding. We could never afford it ... not even a quarter share of such a thing. Surely you can figure it out. We are so ...'

'In debt, I know.' She moved away and snatched a series of tissues out of a box. Flip, flip, flip. She crushed them all over her nose and mouth.

'Your mascara's run.'

'Thank you, Nigel. It's exactly the kind of

observant encouragement I need right now.'

'We got the best deal out of it all – surely you see it.'

'We should ... or maybe *we shouldn't* sign the document. It's not a deal. It's a legacy. When is the notary coming back?'

'Tomorrow. Are you crazy? Harriet – we ... all our problems were solved by Mama's will. We can't not sign!'

'I don't get to sign, Nige – you do.' She gave me a watery glare across the bed, where she had laid out all our folded clothes. 'I can't find one of my brown shoes.'

'I'm going to put the kettle on.'

'We can't talk in the kitchen.'

I stood in the doorway and glared back at her. 'Yes, we can. We can do anything we like. Come and have a cup of tea, and we'll go over our blessings one more time. Come on, darling – you do see it, don't you?'

'I will when I've found my shoe.'

She was so exasperating. So maddeningly sweet and impossible. Luckily, the kitchen was deserted. The fridge contents told me a number of things. I should shop more frugally, and one should blanch chopped vegetables immediately or they go a horrible shade of brown. I threw out several bags and bowls of diced stuff and put the kettle on.

Harriet walked into the kitchen talking. '... this table was where you solved Tad's online course assignment problems. This fridge was your lifeline. The cupboard under the stairs was perfect for Lori's sheet music. Her cello looked fabulous in Mama's sitting room.' She sniffed.

I had to pull some sense into this. If my wife kept me from signing, it would upset everything for everyone, but especially for us. Why she could not see it was beyond me. I gave her a tally of my own. 'The scullery buttresses are crumbling. The rubble wall has come down. The driveway needs resurfacing. Have you any idea what a truckload of gravel would cost *in Florence?* Goodness knows what'll be found when someone goes up in the roof. The ceilings upstairs all drip. Harriet – you could make the list yourself. Sweetheart – think.'

'I am thinking. The room down the passage where the brown chair is – it's fabulous for thinking. The view from the back terrace is ... there should be a pool down there. You know it would be perfect. The back bedrooms in the wing are so gorgeous ...'

' ... and the bathrooms are so dated. All the taps are jammed. Or they drip, leaving green streaks on the enamel ... Harriet!'

'And what's going to happen to all the furniture ...'

'You know the answer to that one.' I splashed hot water onto a generous mound of tealeaves at the bottom of the big old teapot, which I saw had a crack in the lid. Why did I only see such things when I was upset? 'This teapot's had it.'

'No. It's fine. Everything's fine.' She sat diametrically across from me at the big round table. 'It's me who's going funny.'

'What brought it on?' A glimmer of hope appeared. I hoped it did not shine in my words. In my eyes. She had to see reason.

'Tad's going off tonight. He's meeting a bunch of guys, he called them, and they're taking the train right across to somewhere. Can't remember now.'

'But that's great.'

'I know.'

'Lori's moving down to the hostel in Florence – all the orchestra is getting ready for the Mudge ... whatever.'

'*Maggio Musicale*. Darling – it's her life.'

'I know.'

'And we can afford to give them some money, you know. It's not going to break the bank.'

'It's already broken, Nige.' She lay both forearms in front of her in a hopeless gesture and lowered her head. 'These were the two worst, most expensive years of our lives.'

'But they're nearly over. All I need is to get back, get stuck into some job interviews, and when the bequest goes through ... when it's all settled, you'll see. It'll all work out in the end.' I pushed her mug across, and went round to sit next to her with mine.

'But I don't want it to be the end.'

Ah. There it was. I forked shaky fingers through my hair. I needed a cut, and could not wait to get back to London. Realization there was more to Harriet's outburst than I'd thought came through my own preoccupations. 'Okay – out with it, Harriet. Tell me what's wrong. I think I can feel it, in a way. You tell me.'

'How do I know? I don't know specifically. I'm exhausted. We've done little but sit and talk, sit and eat, sit and listen ... and it's worn me right out.'

'It was meant to be a kind of ...'

'Don't say holiday, Nige. Don't say *holiday*.'

I knew what she meant. I knew very well. Unemployed people don't ... can't ... take holidays. I could not wait to get back to London and seek employment. Something had to come up. I was a pretty decent programmer. Some IT firm was bound to offer me something good. Starting on the whole job debacle with Harriet, though, was not a brilliant idea right at that juncture. 'Okay – it's never a holiday with Paola here, is it?'

She nodded and shook her head in turn.

'Having all this – the funeral, the siblings, the family stuff ... all at the same time the kids are getting their wings, their independence ... not easy is it?'

'Nobody needs me anymore.'

There it was again. That's what was wrong with her. The children were drifting away, getting their own lives. We were going to lose our connection to Fiesole. Mama was gone. I had no words. I just stood and pulled the teapot over, and poured myself more tea. 'Drink yours, darling.'

She took up her mug.

'Think of the next two years, Harriet – think of the work. We need to deal with our part of the bequest, and it's going to be time-consuming ... and fun.'

'If everyone signs. We need everyone to sign.'

Did she come out and say it, at last? Relief flooded my head, like a shot of whisky.

'And on top of it all there's lots of organizing to do, and hard work, and changes.'

'Yes, yes, of course.' She saw. I thought she started to see none of it could happen without her.

Brod

Secrets divulged

Nigel and Harriet said they only had about half an hour with Matilde. She was tired, they said, but so very glad to see them. I thought it was because it hadn't been such a long time since they'd seen her that they didn't seem so excited about the visit. They mentioned how well Anna was caring for her, how tiny the flat was, and how difficult it was to park on her street, which was about it.

Later, though, much later, Nigel came down to the back room, where I had thrown myself into Mama's brown armchair. Grant was up in Basile's room tapping messages into his phone and taking photos of the cornicing, or something.

'So are we all leaving at once tomorrow?'

'Paola's staying on, Brod. She said she had no reason, no reason at all, to hurry away.'

'Ah – well ...'

'Yes, Nigel. I guess she can do as she freely pleases.'

He started to sit on the arm of the chair and changed his mind, rising to his full height and moving towards the window. 'The balcony balustrade outside your window upstairs is on its way out.'

'I remember it starting to crumble as a kid – not a surprise.' I smiled. 'Nothing you need worry about. It'll get fixed eventually.'

There was a curious expression on his face, a half-scowl, which he rotated back towards the window again; so close, condensation appeared on the glass. 'Are you fixed for bed linen? Is it warm enough up there?'

'Linen, yes. Heating, not quite. Not a real problem – we're not going to spend much time here, are we? We get on the plane tomorrow … late tomorrow, I think. Has Suzanna been to see Matilde?'

'I think I heard her and Lewis in the hall a minute ago. They've just come back.'

'Listen, Brod. Listen – Matilde … she told me not to tell anyone, but I'm busting to tell, and you're the only one I can say this to. Don't let on.'

'Of course not – what happened?' I could see what happened. I knew. I knew because Matilde had sent me up to the roof space of the back house, where she and Donato had lived, to seek something Mama wanted me to have. 'What did Matilde say, Nigel?'

He shook his head and smiled. 'Do you remember Papa's records? His collection?'

'Hm. I think the records used to be kept in the bottom drawer of the tall bookcase thing in the hall.'

'There were actually heaps more. Lots of vinyl –

some fabulous recordings with Tullio Serafin conducting, boxed sets of operas, complete works of Wagner, Rodrigo, Boccherini ... I mean – some very amazing stuff.'

'And ...'

'And Donato took it all down to Prato, because Mama wanted him too – but he was to use it, care for it, and keep it ... for me. That, and the chess set, for Tad. Since Donato died, since Mama died, Matilde has been keeping them for me. I can't believe it. You do not *know* how music mad we are.'

'Both your kids are musicians, Nigel – everyone knows. Wow – all the records, eh? Good stuff.'

'I always ... well no – there were years I never gave it a thought. I did sometimes wonder where it had all gone. It's a magnificent collection. All in expensive editions. It's not awfully valuable now, but to me, it's priceless.'

'And you get to keep it. Wow.'

'How I'm ever going to get it back to England is another matter, but ... I'm so pleased. You couldn't possibly have any idea how pleased, Brod.'

It was time I took him into my confidence too. 'Matilde gave me a similar surprise, Nigel.'

He took his eyes away from the window for an instant, spun to face the room, and lowered his head. He nodded for a long minute, slowly, took off his glasses, cleaned them without looking, on the hem of his jumper, placed them on his nose again, and stared through them at me. 'Mama was so darned clever. I was starting to worry about having all the records to myself, but ...'

'She ... what I think is ... she wanted us all to

see we weren't just one, two, three, four.'

'One, two, three, four? Oh – I see. To feel we weren't all the same. So she gave us special things, things she knew we'd appreciate, things we wanted.'

'Hm. She got Matilde to get me to climb up into the roof of the little house at the back.' I rose and paced around and back.

'And did you? What was there?'

I sat on the arm of the brown chair. 'Three ... *three* absolutely brilliant Persian rugs. Perfectly cleaned, rolled, expertly packed ... I recognized the patterns. Goodness knows we rolled about on them enough times as kids. They're the ones that used to be down in the dining room, the library, and the big upstairs drawing room. They are immense. I'd forgotten they were so brilliant. Grant was stunned.'

'Does he ...'

'Of course he knows about such stuff. He was completely bowled over. They're good silk rugs, Nigel. I couldn't be more pleased. I feel a bit funny telling you, because Matilde said not to say a word.'

'Well – you know about the records now, and the chess set, so it's fair.' He lifted his chin and thought a bit. 'So do you think the girls ...?'

'Ah!'

'Hah – of course. This is Mama all over.'

I wasn't sure. 'Is it like her? I don't remember her like that at all. Not secretive or scheming.'

Nigel shook his head again. 'No – no, not scheming. Just clever, and wanting to make us happy. Planning gifts. She always planned gifts.'

'Some gift! Three precious Persian rugs. Do you know ...' I stopped short of discussing value. I did not want to bring money into it.

Neither did Nigel. He was circumspect. 'Ha ha. Shall I tell you what I think? I think they'd be easily as valuable as a vast record collection of every bit of recorded music known to ...'

I laughed. 'I have to agree. She was so clever.'

'Mama was something else. The girls will either tell us or they won't, but we can safely say they received something each – something both of them would value as much as you and I value what we got.'

Grant joined us at this point, so conversation split and diverted to other things. It was nice outside. We suggested a walk down to the iron railing over the street, but Nigel stayed behind.

'I told Nigel about the rugs.'

'Oh, yes.' Grant was still intent on his phone.

'We still haven't discussed the whole business of the inheritance with anyone, Grant.'

He looked up, and the expression in his eyes was vague. 'What's to discuss? Too early, I think. Let everyone get used to things. Let some time pass.'

'But do you think everyone will sign the acceptance this evening?'

'Oh – is it this evening?'

'*Grant!* The notary's coming by. He'll need a witness to the signatures. Will you ...?'

'Hmm. Why not? Will the others be okay with it?'

We reached the wrought iron railing, which was choked with runners and weeds. It was still possible to lean over it to see the narrow street below. Yellow-painted houses with dark green shutters bounded both sides as far as one could see down, and up, to a bend where a whitewashed stone wall brimmed with foliage and flowers from what must have been another walled garden. I regarded at it all with some satisfaction. It smelled wonderful in rainy weather. If I had anything to do with it, Mama's villa and garden would stay in the family forever. 'We ought to talk to Paola, though. We must.'

Grant assented absentmindedly, turned his back to the railing, and lifted eyes to the sky.

'Do you know what annoys me about my brother?'

'Nigel?'

'Hmm. He always assumes a monopoly over music. Like he's the only one … like his family's the only family in the world that appreciates and knows about music.'

'His kids are musicians.' Grant looked up from the little phone screen.

'But I mean, the music at the funeral!"

'I thought your mother left a list. A playlist.'

'Good thing she did. We'd have had Gounod and Mendelsohn and the entire Verdi Requiem otherwise.'

'It wouldn't have made a big difference to people like me, Brod. A choir's a choir … you know. Orchestral music is orchestral music.'

I bopped him on the arm. 'You great big Philistine.'

'My music taste is more … enough about my music taste. I can see it makes you angry. D'you know who would make this house absolutely wonderful? Do you know who would plan a smashing renovation? Tristan Horsfield.'

'No!'

He laughed. 'You know he would.'

There was a moment's silence, in which the buzz of a distant motor scooter reached us from below.

'We're going to be pretty busy, Grant.'

He shuffled, moved, pushed shoulders back and smiled.

I didn't need to say a word of explanation.

He smiled again. 'By the time we're finished with our current plans, Brod, we'll be puffed out ...'

'Don't say it.'

'What?'

'Don't say you're growing *old*.'

Grant smiled. 'Ageing is like a neighbour erecting a three-storey house, which obliterates your perfect view of the most beautiful mountain in your country. You know it's coming. You watch the piling of timbers, the arrival of a concrete mixer, delivery of pallets of bricks. In the same way as you watch the first few wrinkles, greying hairs, diminished agility. You know it's coming, but the knowledge doesn't reduce your sorrow. You mourn for the view. You grieve for your youth. You will never again see or photograph the changing colours, the screening of rain, the shafts of summer sun. It was there. You saw it. You will forever grieve its passing. You can't bring it back.'

'When you put it like ...'

He didn't say any more.

I didn't say anything either. I saw what he was saying. There was no time for a family, least of all small babies. I could have said I'd changed my mind;

that I'd thought it over properly, but th
real need.

Something Nigel said made me real
some of what he had; two teenagers whose successes
and futures were an intrinsic part of him and Harriet.
I knew I couldn't have everything. I always wanted
what the others had. All my life. Tonight, though,
something in Nigel's eyes had told me he wouldn't
mind a bit of what *I had*. It was a revelation. No one
had ever envied me; I knew that much. His wife
surely wanted some of what I had recently inherited.

Grant pocketed his phone at last. 'Your niece
and nephew ... they can come and stay whenever
they like. I hope you'll let them know they can.'

I would. I seemed to feel they just might.

Suzanna

Crystal dishes

I didn't know what got into me, but the morning went differently to how I felt it should, and Lewis retreated into himself as usual. It was either Otto's health, or something else – I didn't know. When a dog wouldn't touch his dinner, something had to be wrong.

Dogs sensed tension. I thought the little creature sensed I had started to think differently about the will! He wouldn't touch the wet stuff, or the little biscuits I put into a little glass dish on the kitchen floor.

'This,' Harriet pointed out, without emphasis, without raising her voice, without batting either of her enviable deep eyelids with super-long eyelashes, 'is Bavarian crystal. It's part of Mama's complete set.'

I looked at the dish. Otto looked at it too. He didn't touch a single one of the biscuits. 'I know, Harriet. We've been using those glass dishes since we were little. Matilde used to make us custards and things in them.'

She busied herself with putting cutlery away. 'All right, I suppose. Okay then.'

I almost blurted out to her, there and then, that I'd noticed she was not happy about the house. I almost came out with the fact I'd been thinking about the agreement or acceptance or whatever the document was called, and wondered whether I should sign. I almost stated loudly and clearly I knew she was cut up about having to leave the house, and the grounds, and the garden, and the furnishings, and Mama's complete set of Bavarian crystal dishes. 'When's the notary due?'

'What?' She whirled round, her mouth a pursed oval.

Surely my question was not so surprising! 'I mean – we're all going to start leaving, aren't we? We all have lives to go back to. Work, and a dozen other things. I have a boat to ...' I stopped. Confusion filled my mind. Everything was in utter disorder – my mind was mush. Paying so much for a magnificent boat would not be easy at all if I didn't sign the acceptance.

If one of us didn't sign, it would be as if none of us signed, and the whole thing would turn into a contestation. A contestation! Something so complicated it would take years to dispute and decide and untangle. Lawyers would end up getting much more than we four could ever hope for. I swallowed hard. The house in Cornwall might be lost. All those memories of Papa coming home with the wind in his hair, talking about the tide and the way the wind died or rose or blew or turned whatever. Paola was not the only one with memories. I had my share too.

My ire bubbled up. I told myself I had to be nice to poor Harriet. 'Lewis is so fed up of me he finally marched out for a walk on his own. He didn't even take Otto.'

'Oh! Fed up?'

'I'm being beastly. Maybe... I don't know.'

Harriet went all funny. 'Suzanna, it's grief. We haven't grieved long or deeply enough. Any of us.' She seemed close to tears.

I saw she was struggling with something too. 'Are you all right, Harriet?'

'Not really. Oh!'

What a sigh it was.

'If Nigel was here he'd put the kettle on and think he could fix everything in the world – set everything right and tickety-boo – with a pot of tea.'

'Not such a bad idea.'

She laughed. 'You Larkins are all so different. Yet you're all the same. You all speak with the same rhythms. Even Tad is so much like you all. As changeable as the weather. As steadfast as ... as ... this house.' She filled the kettle with the silly gooseneck tap, which didn't go with anything else in the place, and put it on the stove. 'I think Nigel's all right with the will. Are you all right with the will?'

She could be so direct. It was the most annoying thing about her. I peeked inside Nigel's tin for biscuits. 'I think both the boys will sign. Paola is a bit of a closed box.'

'A bit of an unknown quantity. Hm. You?'

I looked out of the kitchen window. 'Whether I

think it's fair or not, Harriet, signing is definitely the only way to get me my boat, without me having to go into all sorts of financial wrangles. My accountant will cheerfully wring my neck if I ask him anything else this year.'

'But you sold a big franchise or something. It was the very first thing you said when you arrived.'

I bit into a biscuit and noted the way she made the observation. 'Yes, we did. It doesn't mean we'll see the money before three months are up. The way Mama devised the inheritance means I can do everything so comfortably. It's pretty close to unbelievable.'

'And yet ...?'

I sat in the spot – my old spot at our table – which gave me a view over the roof of the little house at the back and the line of trees out by the road. It made me feel all of twelve years old, and just as confused. 'And yet, I hardly feel it's fair.'

'I thought you might be happy with your division.'

Ah. I saw what it was. It was a bit of envy, and resentment. She and Nigel were struggling, and here I was, planning the purchase of a very expensive boat. To her it must have seemed like an impossible luxury. 'My division? It's perfect. Mama knew it was perfect. You know it's perfect. Still, I can't help thinking it's not fair.'

'How can it be perfect and not fair?'

'It's considerably more ...'

She started. 'Oh! You think it's unbalanced ... in your favour.'

She came around the table, lowered her head

to gaze straight into my face, and put her hand on mine. A very unusual thing. Behind her, the kettle was boiling its head off.

'The kettle.'

'Never mind the kettle. I'm not Nigel. Listen, Suzanna – it's dead straight. Fairer than anything in the world. Mama had it absolutely right. Don't feel she didn't. I'm satisfied she did.' Harriet pulled away, twisted the stove knob and poured hot water into the pot. 'Do you like it strong?'

She made what she felt was strong tea, but it seemed pale to me. It didn't matter. What did matter was her reassurance we were all getting what we wanted in the end. I wished Paola would say something similar! And Brod.

I couldn't wait for them to say something without a prompt from me. It would take ages, and Lewis was even now piling things into the car, if I knew anything about him. He liked to be ready ahead of time; organized, organized! He might not be a people person, but he was undoubtedly a *things* person.

Paola and Brod had the most to discuss about the contents of the will, and neither of them had said a word so far. I thought it was Paola's place, as the eldest, to gather us all for a final discussion before the notary arrived to witness us sign the precious piece of paper, which would make it all happen.

I think it's what she had tried to do the previous evening, before we all trooped down to the *osteria*. We all kept talking over what she said, and Nigel came out and said it wasn't the time. What could he mean? What other time was there? We had no idea when all four of us would be in one place again. He was as maddening as his wife!

Perhaps it was up to me. Why was it always up to me? Lewis was right. Everyone else had come to expect it of me over the years.

And what I had to do first, Lewis or no Lewis, siblings or no siblings, was change my shoes and walk down over the uneven paving to the little house at the back. I could leave Otto to his dry kibble in the fancy old bowl for a while. He might work up an appetite on his own. Poor Otto!

One did not bring one's gardening shoes to such a reunion, definitely not to a funeral. I had to put on the oldest pair I brought, with the lowest heels. The little house at the back was only a courtyard's length away. There were slippery patches, because of the recent rain, and a weedy sort of flowering bush erupting in various places through cracks. No doubt Brod would see prettiness in the image. Paola would be distressed and want it all to return to the condition the whole place was in when Mama cared for it. Nigel would consult me, and ask what I thought!

And I would tell him. I'd say this place was not a patch on any house he cared to mention in Newquay, where the boats were visible from the house, and where surfers carried their boards right into the pubs.

Memories of this small servants' house helped, when the paving stopped suddenly at a wall with a tall window in it. Unlike the vast majority of windows in the area, the woodwork here was not the special signature dark green, but a vapid shade of blue. It was evidently sky blue once, but was flaking and faded now. I knew to turn right there and seek the front door down the side. When we were children it was sheltered by an arch covered in white climbing roses. All I saw now was an untidy mass of twigs and thorns, which came close to choking the entire doorway. Someone had cleared an opening very recently, so I could try the handle. The door was locked, but memory served me well, and I reached up as high as I could to the top of the doorway, under the metal lantern, and walked fingers on the narrow architrave ledge, beneath a lethal tangle of thorny twigs.

The key fell to the paving with a single clang. Brown, rusty, it did show scratches where it had not long ago been inserted and twisted.

I was in. The massive chimney breast over the fireplace in the front room was as I remembered it, only there were no Faenza plates hanging off the three hooks any longer. Two armchairs, a small table and a threadbare rug were grouped beside the hearth, and to one side stood an *armadio;* the same white-painted *armadio* I remembered, whose top I could hardly reach as a child. A dull mirror and a bald clothes brush hung on the far wall.

The door to the passage stood open, but the one down the end was closed. Oh! It was as Matilde described. Yes. There it was. Thick curtains at the windows and rush matting on the floor meant it was insulated to a certain extent. Yes! My beautiful bookcase, my Chippendale break-front authentic bookcase was in pristine original condition. It was mine. Mine, mine! So Matilde said. Mama had left her secret instructions, and I was to tell no one.

It was much more beautiful – and larger – than I remembered. The bottom drawer would indeed accommodate a hide-and-seeking child! Brilliant. For some reason it made me very happy. So very content. How could Mama guess I adored it so? It would fit perfectly in our drawing room at home, or the hall, and Lewis would see it stood on level flooring, filled with some of our books. Oh, perfect!

Footsteps in the front room made me turn.

'Is this what Matilde was talking about, when your face lit up earlier?'

'Yes, Lewis. Isn't it beautiful?'

He put an arm around my shoulders and squeezed. 'It will look fabulous in our house. You were right. It's quite a piece. What's such an amazing piece of English furniture doing in an old holiday home in Fiesole?'

'Mama brought all sorts of things from Cornwall. She'd have them crated and sent. She felt nothing in interior décor beat an Italian house furnished the English way.'

'But you preferred it in England.'

'Of course. It's where Papa ... no one even *mentions* him anymore! It's like he's completely out of the picture.'

He pulled me round and embraced me. 'This is grieving time for Mama, sweetheart. It's ... they're ...'

I snuggled into his broad chest, in the way I'd burrow into Papa's. It stopped the tears, the angry tears, which threatened to come.

'It'll soon be time to get on our way. We'll have the bookcase packed and shipped by someone professional, Suzanna – and it will be with us before long. The notary will be here at about noon, and after that, darling, we ought to drive off. For sure.' He paused. 'Are you going to sign?'

'Yes, of course I am.'

'Good. There's all the stuff with the boat to think of. And Otto.'

'Poor Otto.'

'He's getting on, Suzanna.'

'We all are. I thought all us four siblings would be just the same...'

'The same as ever? No one ever is. Everyone changes with age. Relationships change people. You said it yourself. You've changed – I've never seen you so sentimental ... my hard-as-nails wife.'

'Nigel's morphed into another Harriet! Brod still wears awful clothes, and needs a good barber – but he's calmed so dramatically ... if you know what I mean. He's not so envious any more. Then Paola ...'

'She's still in shock, I think.'

'But she's recovering. The will has meant a lot to her.'

'What do you think she'll do?'

'Something tells me she'll never go back to Australia. I mean – she might go back to finish off her life there ... tie up all her ends. I don't know much about writing – but can't authors live anywhere, in fact?'

'I think so. Suzanna – you're freezing. Let's go up to the big house and get Nigel to turn up the heating another notch.'

I laughed. 'Nigel and his notches.'

'I found out what's eating him, as you might

put it.'

We locked the door behind us. I knew Lewis would continue.

'He lost his job.'

'Ah. That's it. Harriet kept talking about a struggle. She made a face whenever I mentioned the boat.'

'They're in a pretty cruel financial situation, with two kids in their most expensive life stage, all this travelling ... caring for Mama, organizing the funeral. He's had a lot on his mind, and is unquestionably frantic about finding a job.'

I did not know what to think or say.

Lewis did. 'He should be in London seeking interviews.'

'He should.'

It was only a matter of hours before the day was done. Goodness knew what would happen when the notary came to the house again.

I could guess Nigel was glad about Mama's division of the '*successione*' and would sign without a murmur, even though Harriet was woefully emotional about losing the Fiesole house. It might still be sold, no matter how cleverly Mama calculated the whole thing. Or would my brother's wife sway him, and urge him to contest, so a 'normal' division would take place at some point, of everything divided equally into four parts?

There was no mystery about what would happen to my plans if it happened; disaster. Mama's plan was perfect for me. My little niggles of doubt about fairness had settled into acceptance. It's amazing what an hour can do to one's mind – and finding the bookcase added to my contentment. It was easy to let matters flow according to my mother's astute proposal.

It left Paola, of course. If Paola made up her mind about something, nothing and no one could move her. It's what she was always like. Slow, steady, silent and stubborn! Mind you, I saw a distinct softening in her, a hesitancy I had never seen before. The end of a marriage could do that to a person. Couldn't it? It was not easy to guess what it might do. I had seen various friends – male and female – through break-ups, but watching a sibling suffer is something else altogether. I thought I knew my big sister so well – and she became a bigger mystery since I saw her last.

Which was when? Memory failed me. It was a shame we didn't meet more often. We were flung to various distances, and geography can be a tyrannical – a despotic – thing.

I knew what I had to do – make everyone promise we would have reunions every few years, and not leave the next meeting for another funeral! They would boo and hiss if I put it quite in those words. I had to find the words.

Paola

Oranges

I knew what it was; it came to me after a while. People changed. They changed very radically when their mother died. We all transformed into people other than ourselves; it might have been into our true selves, when Mama died. John said something like it once but I didn't believe him. I never believed him when he made observations about the family.

'Women whose mothers are still alive stay girls. You're still a girl, Paola, even in your fifties. There's always someone there you can run to.'

I was annoyed with him for some reason at the time, but I had to admit now, while listening to the sounds of the others packing all around me, while I fidgeted with things in my funny little damp room – trying to make sensible decisions – that he had been right, all those years ago.

Suzanna had mellowed, and more so since the funeral. Now she was going about telling everyone we should meet more, and not leave it until it was an emergency. She didn't say, 'Let's not wait until somebody dies!' But it was what she meant. Her exclamations echoed around the house. She moved with a bit more assurance and was a great deal more comforting than in the past, when all she wanted to be good at was out-doing everyone. She seemed a bit less confident her boat purchase would work. It was lovely to see her take advice from anyone who had anything to say about it.

Nigel was more distant. He no longer acted like master of ceremonies, the monarch of all he surveyed. It was almost as if he no longer had to make up for being the youngest. It might have been because he was the only one of us who was a parent. Raising Lori and Tad could not have been easy, but he and Harriet had reason to be proud. I could see my little brother was taking leave of Fiesole, going from room to room, and trailing through the long grass at the back, saying farewell not only to the place but also to his childhood.

I wondered, while folding my coloured shawl for the third time, whether it was Grant who had transformed Brod. Poor Brod; he felt Mama's death the most, and was most prey to his own emotions, but something had strengthened him. His face was the one of a man who had made an important decision. Mama's apron strings were well and truly severed. I wondered how often he had consulted her on matters going on in his life. I knew he communicated often with her – possibly more than any of us. Now, he was down in the cellar boxing wine, all on his own, chewing at memories and happinesses and regrets. Communing with our mother's ghost.

Grant was still taking pictures of the back bedrooms, and the exterior of the scullery, with a real camera this time, not his phone. He worked slowly, and I had no doubt he would come up and show me. A month ago, when I was still so falsely strong and steady within what I thought was a permanent relationship, I would have found his behaviour overly sweet, a bit too charming. Today, I saw both Brod and Grant with different eyes. They worked well together; they calculated and analysed, and I liked that. I liked how they had an artistic bent, something aesthetic in the things they liked.

Had I changed? Transformed into someone a bit harder; more capable of analysis ... practical exploration of people and situations? Of course I had. It was less because John had left so suddenly, and without notice. And more because I felt I was completely autonomous at last. No one to look after; and no one to look after me. Even Mama was gone. The sensation was so overwhelming it took days to register properly. Since I surfaced, on my own, with John far away not only in sheer distance, but also emotionally, and intellectually, and practically, I could see my world, and my way through it, a bit more clearly.

It would even come into my writing. I would experiment with other genres. I would write a contemporary novel with a realistic view into changing relationships; morphing marriages.

One decision was set. I would stay on at the villa. There was no rush to get back anywhere. The house in Melbourne was secure, and in any case, it would only take a phone call to get a friend to see to things there. I booted up the laptop and sought maps and train timetables and fares. It was all of a sudden quite exciting to be making solo plans. Sitting with Grant and Brod at the kitchen table had opened up a whole new vista to me.

'No more tea, please. Let's have a glass of the Bramduardi wine.' I diced some provolone Nigel had in the fridge, and slit open a vacuum-packed bag of spiced olives. The three of us sat around the round red table. It was still the warmest room in the house. Cosy, welcoming. It was easy to imagine Matilde making herself busy around us, cleaning the paintwork around the window shutters, her damp rag squeaking, everything smelling of yellow soap. She would pour herself a glass of Cynar.

'Do you remember Matilde drinking Cynar?' Brod brightened.

'What's Cynar?' Grant was curious.

'It's a powerful Italian liqueur made from globe artichokes.' Brod laughed at his partner's grimace.

'Artichokes!'

'It's quite good. Surprisingly good. Matilde would douse it with a good spurt of soda water, squeeze in a twist of orange, and sip it slowly, while she took on her evening's chores.' He nodded. 'Yes, I remember.'

'Oranges from the stunted tree behind their house. Blood oranges from the south, she called them. I wonder if the tree's still there.'

'There was a little grove of all kinds of citrus trees. I remember the blossom. Donato would trim off branch ends full of blossom, and Mama would put them in the hall vase.'

The memory of the scent was powerful in the warm kitchen. If Brod and Grant were not there, I would have lain my head in my arms and taken a nap in the imagined scent, on that table, as I had as a thirteen-year old, exhausted after reading all night. I mightn't have changed at all.

But Brod was excited, and wanted to discuss things once more. 'Are you sure it'll all work out, Paola?'

I had to smile. The wine warmed me from the core outward; possibilities offered by the future warmed me from the exterior – from the whole villa – inward. What could I say? 'I don't know, Brod. I could crumble, like this place is bound to do if nothing's done.'

'Mama guessed we'd sit here and debate things. She must have pictured us making tentative plans, a matter of days after Dottor Ugobaldi read us her will.'

I thought of her sitting in the brown chair down the steps, looking out upon the view between treetops, taking a breather before she took on some other task, or before getting us together for a board game. 'Of course she knew. She planned it ... and we're all promptly doing what she planned for us.'

'You – all of you – examined it and turned it all up, down and sideways, though. You all had doubts.' Grant made his point.

'She knew it too.'

Mama didn't know I would attend her funeral alone. She could not possibly foretell what would befall me on the day Nigel called. She could have no suspicion, no doubt, no idea my greatest desire, if I had one at the time, would change so radically. Coming back to the house we called home, coming back to her, was coming back bereft emotionally.

There were things Mama could not predict.

Nigel

A diamond ring

We came here full of hesitation and sadness. Harriet had talked the entire way about how nothing would be the same at the villa without Mama.

'She was at the hospice a long time, Harriet – we looked after things for months.'

She had to agree. It was in her eyes. 'Yes. Just us – I sometimes get rather angry about it. Apart from the odd visit, your brother and sisters did next to nothing. But you're right, it all ran like she wanted it to run. Remember – we even asked her about the kitchen and scullery taps. We had to describe what we were going to install. She was intrigued by the gooseneck thing, and said how she'd have liked such a useful appliance, to rinse out pots and spray olives ready for pickling ... or whatever.'

'She planned everything. She stayed in control ... but was she controlling? I don't think she was controlling, Harriet.'

Now, in the house, getting ready to leave, she made me wonder what magic Mama put into play, to make things go the way she imagined was right. Was she controlling?

'No. Even as children, she let us come to our own conclusions without pushing us. Simply showing us.'

'Was it what the will did? Did it show us?'

'Hmm.' Most of my hesitation was gone. To follow Mama's plan for me was the most sensible and functional option. My precarious financial situation could be wrested into some sort of equitable position without much bother, and Harriet and I could redress our future. The kids were becoming independent, and I could see us enjoying ourselves in a couple of years or so.

'We can fix most things, Harriet.'

'Most things. I'm starting to regret selling my engagement ring.' Her eyes met mine in a timid gaze.

It did not suggest a quarrel was coming on, so I took up the thread. 'It was an impetuous thing you did, Harriet.'

'But ...'

'But well-meant. You were scared of the pickle we were in. You thought a few thousand would fix it. All I could feel at the time was what the ring meant to you ... how we chose it together, how we planned and saved. Years of ... whatever.'

She swallowed. 'We had such an enormous row about it.'

'Well – I was offended and surprised ... look, I'm sorry I hurt you.'

'You always said every little bit helps, so I sold it, and it hardly made a dent in our debt.'

'You should have told me.'

'I wanted to help.'

'You know something?'

She rotated awkwardly away from the window.

'You did help. You did.'

'No – nothing helped, Nigel. You were so angry – so upset.'

I took her hand to examine the little diamond ring I had replaced it with, on impulse, trying to fix small things and big things with one quick purchase. 'I guess this little thing means a lot to us now.'

'We threw good money after bad, I think.'

'Don't say that.'

'No.'

We embraced, in front of the enormous glass windows in the brown room. 'Let's walk down to the little house.' She dug her chin in my chest, as she would so many years before. Now, the hesitation and sadness we arrived with were dissolving into something else I could not quite define.

Many things had changed, but some things stayed the same. Harriet and Paola would only ever tolerate each other. I was used to it. Suzanna would always be self-centred and over-confident.

Although everyone said the funeral went well, I could tell they were grateful I organized everything. It saved them the bother. So I supposed it did go well, despite my horror at the details I could not control. Now it was behind me, sadness enveloped everything to do with it, and I knew sorrow would be the prevailing emotion, not resentment.

Everyone felt calmer and more resigned to things as they were. There was no more talk of refraining from signing the document. Dottor

Ugobaldi would soon sit in the very same place where he'd read the will.

The prim, precise notary had given us *un paio di giorni*, a couple of days, to make our decisions, without a doubt knowing there was no wiser way than our mother's to divide what was in effect indivisible. So one of the last things we would do before we all left on our separate ways was sign. Paola, Suzanna, Brod and I, signing a piece of official paper for the sake of convention, convenience, Italian bureaucracy none of us wanted any part of, but which governed almost every aspect of our lives at the house, and Mama's.

She insisted on drawing up an Italian will. It must have been important to her. So here we were, all willing to partake in her meaningfulness whether we understood it or not, for her sake, who had done so much for us. Even if it was days after we'd learned how she wanted it to go.

'I never understood her completely, Harriet – you became closer to her after all the years.'

'Mama understood you four perfectly well. She was vague and muddled towards the end, but it didn't take away her understanding of all of you. Not as *the children*, all in one lump or clump. Individually – even Brod and Suzanna.'

'Especially Brod and Suzanna. She never bundled them together, as some do with twins.'

The little citrus grove behind the little house where Donato and Matilde lived was overgrown and neglected. Fallen fruit and leaves formed a mushy mat underfoot, and the unpruned trees appeared twiggy and plaintive against the grey sky.

'Lemons, mandarins, blood oranges ...' Harriet pointed at the trees, stepping hesitantly between them. 'Look at all this wasted fruit. Lovely plump winter lemons ... and do you remember eating oranges and mandarins Matilde had somehow preserved? How did she do it?'

I tried to remember. 'I don't think we ever thought about it. She'd call us down to the grove, spread out an old blanket, sit us down, and hand us each an orange or mandarin wrapped tightly in paper. Waxed paper. I remember its smell and how it crinkled, and how Brod would ball all the pieces up and we'd have a paper ball fight.'

Harriet smiled. 'She must have delayed picking as long as she could, and carefully wrapped each fruit, packed it all tightly ...'

'... in crates. Yes, I remember. Crates – and she'd hand us each a fruit every day.'

'You had two mothers, in effect, lucky thing.'

I saw she was thinking of her own disadvantaged childhood, brought up by a distracted aunt after a road accident robbed her of both parents in one night.

'They welcomed you with open arms, Harriet – both of them, Mama and Matilde.'

'Yes. Lovely, comforting. I did feel welcome, of course I did. But I was twenty-one or something. I've missed a lot in life. No one ever gave me a wrapped orange, or drove me all over the place to pools and things as a child. Or woke me up early on a Sunday with specially made pancakes. Gosh – you lucky thing!'

'You did it for *our* kids.'

Her smile was priceless. 'Of course. Lori's pancakes with blueberries, and Tad's with honey and lemon juice ... I learned such a lot from Mama.'

I knew what she meant. For a minute, we were both quiet, no doubt contemplating the same thing; aspects of Mama's care, attention and thoughtfulness.

'The statue we saw at the cemetery - a beautiful woman with her face lowered into her hand.'

'What a splendid sculpture.' Neither of us had seen it before.

'Yes – but I imagined it was Mama, feeling sorry she had to leave. Silly, but it was what I felt.'

'I thought it was a bit like Matilde. She didn't come to the funeral. She grieved at home. She wanted to remember Mama as she knew her. No cypresses, no hearse, no burial.' I tugged at an orange from the few left on the low branches around us, and peeled it quickly. A blood orange. Its red segments came apart easily. The taste was magic. A throw-back to sunny summer days of hastily shed waxed paper, oranges shucked of their orange hide, and Matilde watching, with an expression on her face which was indecipherable to children.

Standing in the little citrus grove was a kind of farewell.

I put an arm around her shoulder. 'We can always visit, Harriet.'

She smiled and chewed on juicy orange segments I handed her. 'I don't know about always, but yes, we'll be back.'

Suzanna

Skipper

Driving away was a touch sad. It was all over; the funeral, meeting the family, telling everybody about our plans and things! Exciting in a way, to be able to plan so much more comfortably now.

Lewis had the car waiting, all packed, with Otto wagging his tail, peering over the back seat. My husband stood with his back to me, fingers loosely at the door handle. He wanted to go.

'Off we go, Lewis. All is ahead of us now.'

'All thanks to Mama and her vision, Suzanna.'

'I guess!'

He was quiet for a moment, putting the car in gear and allowing it to freewheel a bit down the uneven drive. The crunch of gravel was punctuated every now and then by some larger lump of soil or rock under the wheels.

'You guess?' He talked without making eye contact.

'Hmm?'

'Did you say all your goodbyes all right?'

'Yes.'

'Excited about the boat?'

I took a deep breath. 'Do you realize Mama's foresight puts us in a position to be able to drop everything and go sailing for good and all, Lewis?'

It was his turn to nod. 'Of course I do. What I'm not sure of is whether I *want* to drop everything.'

Oh. He had had the opportunity to do a lot of thinking on his own. It was plain on his face, whose profile I peered at in the grey light. Grim mouth, and crows-feet creases at his eyes as he squinted at the road ahead. I wanted to exclaim, *Lewis!*

But I didn't. This was no time to hurry him along. It would be hell afloat to be trapped on a boat with a reluctant partner; one who did not want to be there. The success of our adventure relied heavily on both of us being comfortable and happy with our plans. Both of us willing to cast off wholeheartedly and sail away content.

When had I started to see this clearly? When I considered poor old Paola. Devastated and astounded by the premature ending of her marriage. I saw in her what unpleasant surprises could do to a woman in her fifties; set her immobile and unfulfilled on a difficult spot to move from. I didn't want it to happen to me!

'No surprises, Lewis. Tell me what's actually on your mind.'

'Really?'

'Really truly!'

Not having to look me in the eye gave him the freedom to speak plainly, driving down into

Florence, his eyes firmly on the road. I was so glad we set off early, before the traffic grew bad.

'Suzanna, my greatest fear is the prospect of living in the strict confines of a boat with you acting like skipper. Captain. Boss.' He did the Larkin thing of giving three names to the one thing. It was a long sentence for Lewis. Long and specific.

'I won't ...'

'Yes, you will. It would wreck everything. I know we won't always be on the boat. I know we'll be home a lot too, but I don't want to spend the rest of my days as galley slave.'

'Lewis!'

'So I've decided something.'

My heart sank. In one or two sentences, Lewis dashed my hopes and plans. There were no words to describe my crushed feelings. I sat back in the seat, lay my head against the rest, and closed my eyes.

'Are you listening, Suzanna?'

'Yes.'

'I'm going off to take a course. I intend to get my skipper's ticket. On someone else's boat, in my time, at my pace.'

I sat up. 'What?'

'When we step on board *Char-à-banc*, if we do get her, I want to be skipper. I know you're the sailor, you're the one with the dream. I have a dream too, though, and I won't let it take second place to yours.'

My voice was low. I could hear poor old Otto panting in the back. 'O – *kay*.'

Lewis smiled. 'Okay. Yes. Okay, so – we'll both be skippers, and we'll take our adventure in turns. In stages. Stages I can handle – at my pace.'

'Goodness, Lewis – you can give a girl a shock.'

He laughed. He knew he had slowed me in my reckless rush towards my brand of adventure. Put the brakes on a bit. Added a bit of caution!

'When you signed the succession acceptance document a minute ago ...'

I looked at my watch. 'It's two hours ago. I can't believe it.'

'Yes, we'll take the ring road and be away from Florence quite soon. When you signed that paper, Suzanna, it sort of sealed our fate.'

I laughed at his ominous words. 'Oh, Lewis. Lighten up!'

'Yes. I will. You lighten up too. Let's not hurtle into this – I want us to take our time. We'll do all the sailing you like. I don't doubt for a minute we'll get *Char-à-Banc*. Mama made it all so much easier. Let's not go too fast.'

I put my hand on his thigh, on his unfaded new jeans. 'Anything you say, Skipper.'

Brod

An unusual revelation

Grant was downstairs helping Paola plan her trip to Naples. I knew why she was going, now she said a sentence or two about it. She was never one for going into too much detail. Besides, I saw there were obvious personal reasons she did not want to go into. Grant, however, was a very intuitive guy. Which was one of the reasons he always saw through me. I used to mind, but when I realized it was because he was interested in me and my thoughts and views, and how I did things, and that it was not an issue when it took a long time to make up my mind about something, it was fine.

Grant was a complex person, and his subtle way of observing things, saying neutral sentences instead of cutting personal statements, seemed quite charming; until people saw how clever he was. And caring. He missed his calling, and should have been a psychologist. Some sort of therapist.

'Design is therapeutic, and very personal, Brod.

I responded to the call. I love working with people.'

What he was doing with Paola was not work, though. He saw her as family. It was a compliment to me as well as to her.

'The train is the best idea, you're right.' His fingers trailed the map. 'And when you get here ...'

She glanced up at him from Mama's brown armchair. 'You do know why I'm going to Naples, don't you?'

Grant tilted his head. 'We both do, Paola. You're going to visit Basile Sottalbero.'

'His grave.'

'Are you sure Matilde gave you the right details?'

'She gave me an address. I have someone to search for ... his grandniece. Her name is Beatrice Sottalbero, and she lives in the Vomero district.'

'Wow. Fancy.'

Paola fixed surprised eyes on Grant. 'You know Naples?'

'I visited on holiday with my parents.'

I waved a finger at him. 'I thought you said they never took you anywhere!'

'This was a disaster they weren't willing to repeat.' He laughed. 'Years and years ago. We stayed halfway up the hill, underneath the Vomero, and had quite nice views. I don't remember much – but my people did say the Vomero was home to the upper middle class.' He took a deep breath. 'Snobs, they were, Mum and Dad. A bit supercilious and upwardly mobile – more concerned about what people thought than how things affected me, in fact.'

This was an unusual revelation. It clarified

things for me to see Grant confiding in Paola.

She smiled and went on about the artist's grandniece in Naples. 'Matilde said she paints too.'

'Oh? Have you looked her up?'

I saw it hadn't occurred to Paola. Her laptop was quickly unfolded and she tapped and scrolled until she found something. 'Well – come and see at this. She's got a good website. Apparently quite successful ... and she's won awards.'

'What's her work like?'

She swivelled the computer so we all could see.

Grant and I looked at each other, then at Paola. 'Rather good. Very active. See what she does a lot of?'

'I know.' Paola was not about to jump to conclusions or decisions. 'I know what you're thinking, Brod.'

Grant asked for the laptop to be twisted around. 'Very interesting. Is this anything like what her uncle used to paint?'

'No, not similar at all. I can't see any of his vision there. You never know, though. Beatrice Sottalbero seems to be more decorative and less conceptual ... quite realistic, I would say. Technically quite good.'

'Well – one has to be, if one paints *trompe l'oeils*. Are you thinking what I'm thinking?'

We all gave signs of agreement. Grant tilted his head. 'Well, have a lovely time in Naples, whenever you plan to go. It might ... You might ...'

Paola stood and smoothed the front of her long skirt. 'Yes – I might and I might not find her. And if I do, we might not hit it off.'

'True. In any case, good luck.'

Her hand wavered. 'Are you two leaving soon?'

'We have to. Grant has a project coming up in London. I should get back to the bank before they toss me out.'

Grant laughed. 'Not much chance of it happening. You're right, though, we should get back, now all the papers are signed and everything's in place.'

I rubbed my chin. 'Must shave before we go. Do you think Nigel was right about the moustache?'

Grant and Paola responded together. 'Yes!'

'So why didn't anyone tell me ... oh. All right.' He laughed. 'How long do you think it will be before the succession is settled?'

'The notary said a matter of a few weeks. Everything was so well-planned and organized. Mama has well and truly vaulted Italian bureaucracy.'

'It's what I thought when I saw the striking statue at the cemetery – the one down the avenue, where ...'

'The woman with her head in her hand.'

'Oh?'

I went on. 'Yes. I thought – it's Mama thinking. Contemplating, planning how to leave us a fair division without us having to fight, choose, sort out, come to divisions ourselves.'

'I thought the statue was about deepest grief.'

I half-agreed with my sister. 'Yes and no. I saw Mama thinking. It's a beautiful statue.'

She did not say anything.

'Listen, Paola. When you find Beatrice ... I mean – if you do like her, tell her about our frescoes.

Tell her about the wall gods, how we'd like them restored.'

'Wouldn't it be fantastic?' Grant's eyes left the window.

She agreed. 'It would. I have this vision of those walls brightening, coming back to what they once were. The hall would be transformed.'

'I have dreams about how this place could look one day. Look and feel.'

'So do I, Brod. So do I!' My sister rearranged her shawl, picked up her laptop and book, and climbed the four steps back to the kitchen.

I watched her go, wondering whether it would all work out the way I imagined it would.

'Come on,' Grant said. 'We can't take all evening to pack.'

I called after Paola. 'What's going to be done about transferring utilities ... all that? What'll ... um?'

Her face was calm. 'Dottor Ugobaldi has it all down pat, Brod. I'll return from Naples in a few weeks, and it'll all be done. He is without question as efficient as he seems.'

I thought he conceivably had a staff of six. But she was right.

Grant and I talked in the car on the way down to the ring road around Florence. The traffic was dreadful, but Grant was the most patient of drivers, which is why I left it to him.

'So do you think it will work, Brod? I'm getting excited about it all.'

'I think so. Mama left the Fiesole villa to Paola and me, just us two, for a reason. We're the two most likely to keep it and restore it properly. I don't think it would have been the same if John were still in the picture. He's not, however. Mama could not have known it. She knew Paola and I would see eye to eye.'

'For sure?'

'Oh, most definitely. Paola's finding her feet, and looking forward to living in the villa, for good.'

Grant smiled broadly. 'And did you like her idea about the little house at the back?'

'Well – didn't you? It would suit us so well. It will be gorgeous when it's done up. You will have a great time doing that. Also, we might very well have an artist for the frescoes.'

'I could see a coat of arms painted on the chimney breast in the small house.'

I laughed. 'See? I knew you'd love this. It's fabulous we don't have to buy anybody out. Mama's magic.'

'Paola's idea, of running a retreat for writers from all over the world, of hosting conferences and workshops ... do you think it would work?'

'Hard work ... I can see it happening. It's still far in the future. We'll have to concentrate on the renovation first.'

His forehead creased. 'I was so surprised she did not baulk at the cost. If we go halves on everything, it will work out to be quite reasonable, precisely like she said, but it's still quite a lot of money. You and I can manage, without a doubt, but what about your sister ... ?'

'I told you she was the most likely of us to be able to afford it.'

Paola

Christmases

My plan to visit Naples on my own fitted in perfectly with everything else. All my siblings were quite ready to leave the villa. It was plain they had had a sufficiency of contact with me and each other. They all started moving out, having signed the final document, packed, and said their farewells. Some resentment and awkwardness was still in the air. Things were always stilted in Larkin goodbyes. We never quite got it right.

We lied about how we felt. We lied about what we saw in each other. We lied about the past, and the future. Truthfulness died long before Mama went, but it was benign mendaciousness; it was something we all recognized and accepted. To experiment with honesty was disruptive and dangerous. We could not all be Harriet. We bade our farewells to her with good grace, I supposed.

Suzanna and Lewis were off quickly, thanks to his organized packing. I went up to them in the hall, where my sister had stood her perfect burgundy handbag on the round table.

'Well, then, Paola! Goodbye and ... goodbye. Ciao.'

I had to ask. 'Suzanna – do you remember being given a box of sweets, which converted into a jewel box when we were little?'

She grimaced like I had gone completely mad. 'A jewel box? Full of sweets? No, Paola. Was there ever such a thing?'

I waved a hand, as if to dismiss some flighty butterfly wavering into the hallway. 'Nothing. No. Um ... forget it. Goodbye.'

She kissed me on both cheeks and was gone.

It was a bit distressing, but we all were affected by the last meeting with Notaio Umberto Ugobaldi. That could have been it.

The notary was businesslike as usual. Only one thing he said was cause for regret. He looked at us in turn, and regarded the papers in front of him. His spectacles glinted; the weather had suddenly changed, and shafts of sunlight came through the large windows. 'There was an intention, on the part of your mother, Nina Larkin, to write a letter to each of you.'

There was a combined intake of breath. I could see eager expressions in Brod's, Suzanna's and Nigel's eyes. My heart stopped at the thought of reading a letter from Mama.

'But I am afraid her infirmity overtook her, before she could tackle the task. She left it too late. However, I am very sure you each might imagine what she had to say. Her legacy is obvious – her will was fair. It is abundantly clear she left you more than mere material things. In these envelopes, I have folded a photocopy of some notes she made. They are practically illegible. They are nonetheless yours.'

No letters. We were all disappointed. There was nothing one could do about some of life's omissions.

I watched them go, either from the balcony outside the upstairs drawing room, or from the front steps. It felt good to wave them off. It gave me a new sense of propriety, of being in charge. Of owning something which didn't have anything to do with John. There would be a divorce settlement, but it didn't matter much to me how the split went now. My future was pretty much decided by Mama's wise thinking. Running a retreat for writers in this rambling house would be good, especially if it was done up well. I could rely on Brod and Grant to get the renovation right. The expense would not be a bother – the details would be taken care of without the need to economise or compromise. It would be beautiful when finished.

Brod said something about Mama's exceptional rugs, so I had no doubt he'd got them squirreled away somewhere, to be returned to their original places as soon as ladders, scaffolding, debris and all the mess was cleared away.

How long would it all take? I wondered. Neither I nor Brod and Grant were in a real hurry ... and yet we were eager to start it and see it to completion within a reasonable timeframe.

My next task was to look up Beatrice Sottalbero. I knew I'd be seeking resemblances and differences to her great uncle Basile. I knew I'd trail all over Naples seeking his work to examine and link to memories I had of him. It would tie a loose end which had flown and fluttered, untied, for far too long.

I had two photographs – one of Papa, and one of Mama, taken in Cornwall, which I wanted to be copied, converted into matching oval paintings. I might very well find Beatrice and she could fit the bill, and take on a commission, on my visit to Naples. It would mean a complete break from my Melbourne life, but a continuation to what I'd found here in Fiesole. My old self.

I made a resolution last night – to spend time in Cornwall too. And Wales – my desire to visit Wales had never been entertained, let alone fulfilled, when John was around. Strangely, so strangely, I wanted the rest of my life's Christmases to be English ones, just like the ones of my youth and childhood. Not strictly to recapture anything – or even to cancel the Australian Christmases I'd had – but to fulfil a wish for red and green and silver. A wish for cold weather, churches lit up with more than mere light. Choral music, boots and scarves, and the rich smell of oranges, plum pudding, and real English baking. I needed the music of Byrd and Elgar and Holst – they didn't only belong to Nigel.

I wanted to look out from a window and see the sea, the sea of England. It didn't hold significance only for Suzanna. I might not be the boating kind, but I wanted the sea within walking distance, and renting a cottage in Truro or Penzance was not out of the question.

Before he left, Brod pushed two sheets of paper into my hand.

'What's this?'

He smiled. What a difference shaving off that silly moustache made. It took years off him. 'It's a receipt. From a place down in Florence. They know about you. I've paid for a consignment of seedlings, plants ... little saplings and shrubs and stuff. You can call them and name what kinds you want. I thought ...'

'Brod – this is wonderful of you.'

He beamed. 'Just as wonderful as you giving the Brigante portrait of Papa to Suzanna.'

It was something I had to do.

'When you get back from Naples, Paola, dig your hands in the villa soil. Do what Mama did. Get the garden thriving and splendid again.'

I didn't think Brod would ever know how significant it was, and how it laid out a path for me – a path down through the Larkin history in that rambling place. There was no doubt in my mind the next few years would be gloriously busy, with things I loved doing best.

I had a lot to look forward to in Fiesole.

Nina Larkin

The end

A year ago I sat down to write this. It was still too early. Now, my hand shakes, but I can see my way clear, and I ought to write these notes at some point. There is clarity in writing. Even if only to get it all right in my mind, and base a letter to each of the children on what I scribble here. Yes, I shall do it – a letter each. Or perhaps not? I don't know.

The light comes through these big windows like it always has, but this year something's different. It can't be the sun. It can't be the season. It can only be me. I'm changing, and I know why. I've noticed changes, and they aren't for the better.

Soon, I'll need looking after, round the clock. It's not a nice prospect, but there's nothing I can do to stop my decline. Like there was little I could do when Roland died. I've been a widow longer than we were married, and it still irks and chafes. Time numbs pain, but it cannot take away what was. It cannot erase what could have been. It was so close to perfect it could not possibly last. Perfection is momentary. A flash.

Roland was the beginning and end of everything – but we had four children, wonderful ... dynamic. So full of his spirit. So full of his ideas and verve. Two even inherited his sticky-out ears and clownish smile. One received his observation; another, his sympathy and kindness. The children kept Roland alive. They made his life real. I poured mine into theirs.

I've written to the notary, and he will be here on Monday to take my dictation. We'll do it the old way – I shall speak, and he will write. Umberto will like the sentiment. He liked the way I asked him to be present after my last general check-up at the doctor's. He was satisfied as to the soundness of my mind – we all laughed about it, and I made sure I laughed the heartiest, since I was the case in point. The doctor and nurse signed the 'soundness' papers, which serve only to reassure Umberto Ugobaldi. I've known him for years, and he knows that in about a month, after I am absolutely sure the will is worded correctly, and after he has seen it's lodged with the right authorities, Nigel and Harriet will come to stay.

They were brilliant when they helped me move from Cornwall. It went smoothly enough, and I had made sure the crates I wanted moved were moved at the right time and to the right places. I could not die in Cornwall. It would be too heartbreaking to leave from the same door as Roland. His sudden death was such a shock I could hardly enter the house when I returned from the hospital without him.

Without him. How empty it all was. How hollow and startlingly bare my life would have been if I didn't pick myself up right away and think about the children. Four children, all needing me in their funny little ways ... their urgent, momentous life-changing ways ... and I was all on my own to do it.

As it happened, it worked out very well, and I was only in the Cornwall cottage when it was full of the children's Christmas cheer. We had brilliant summers here in Fiesole, and I did my travelling, painting, and living in between. At the time, it all seemed complicated and not a little scary, especially the first year after Roland went. I did it, however, I did it properly; and I knew the entire time Donato and Matilde had a lot to do with the family's success.

For almost five years, Basile Sottalbero was in my life ... and not. On and off. He hated one part of it; the inconsistency and my lack of commitment, my defiance of seriousness. Such a grave and solemn man. For an artist, he was pretty serious and dependable. He did not understand my English humour, so I was not entirely surprised he grew dismayed with my inability to settle with him forever. No matter how committed, no matter how artistic, no matter how he liked the children, no one could take Roland's place. I said it so many times, in two languages. Basile finally understood, and did not return to the villa the following summer. His last words were about Paola. I laughed. 'Will you miss my daughter more than me, Basile?' Even that was too impenetrable a joke for him.

But he was right to miss my perceptive Paola. She was the only one to notice he was not there the following year. She was the one who needed him most, who most closely observed the way he painted, his attentiveness to detail. And it was likely she saw more than I did. Now, with the benefit of hindsight, I feel her juvenile adoration was a bit more than a young crush. Ah – we tend to think first love is easily brushed off. No – for someone as solemn as Paola, it could possibly have formed her entire life view. Is it possible I only see this now?

How quickly they grew and took off. Now, it's over, and even though Roland's been gone more than forty years, I still long for him, and wish he could see them. His Suzanna, so clever in business. Nigel, so quick to anger, such a thoughtful father, and so easy to appease and please. Brod, in his young confusion – something Roland never knew I would have to contend with, a gay son – who grew up to be a banking brain. He would have marvelled too at Paola's writing talent. No one guessed she would make a living from writing. Her youthful indecision and eloquent excuses developed into an insightful way with words.

I shall leave them everything, but first, the small details. I need to care for Matilde, who was as deeply sorrowful after Donato died as I was about Roland. We always understood each other, Matilde and I. I'll see her flat in Prato is fully paid off, what little there is left to pay, and she will not have a worry in the world for the rest of her days. I shall do it now, simply by writing a cheque, so it is not in any way included in the will.

My lucky strike when inheriting my father's fortune was his flair for investments. I left everything as it was, and took the right advice. I preserved what was there, and some parts grew in value. Roland's flutters in the hospitality industry were surprisingly quite successful, despite his bad timing and crazy ideas, so few dents were made. I remember smiling at his often-repeated assertion. 'Your father's money is family money, and not to be put on a horse!' His ventures were not the same as a mere wager, of course.

I shall leave the Fiesole house to Paola and Brod, together. They are both thoughtful and sentimental enough to keep it. Oh, this house needs to stay in Larkin hands. I do realise it will need restoration, but they will manage. Although I do not think John is in love with Italy, Paola will see she gets enough time here. I often wonder if my big girl and her husband see eye-to-eye, and if the loss of that baby had anything to do with John's occasional coolness. I realized what had happened, even though she did not confide in me. A woman who has had five pregnancies and four children can recognize the effect of loss in a woman's eyes. She never saw I knew, but I did, and had to keep quiet.

I have every confidence that Brod will eventually find someone who understands him, who hopefully will see his fine spirit and warm sentiment. He has great empathy, and a wonderful way in the garden, even if the soil makes him sneeze and gets in his eyes.

Together, or in turns, they will restore the villa back to the way it was when we all enjoyed it. Who knows – they might even entertain guests in the way their father wanted to.

To Nigel and Harriet, who cared for me so well, and spent so much of their time and money bringing me here from Cornwall, I shall leave the cottage in Newquay. Entirely free of encumbrances, it will provide them with a home, and they can dispose of their London flat later, when Lori and Tad finish their studies. It is by far greater than a quarter of the legacy, but Nigel and Harriet made me very comfortable and respected my wishes, without stopping to think about their own inconvenience. It's about time they were recompensed.

I wonder what the notary will think when I tell him the share portfolio is to go to Suzanna? It is a nice little earner. I have done some estimates, and it is worth about two-thirds the value of the Cornwall cottage. So it's very fair. Suzanna can either save it up, or use the income, or put it all towards one of her ventures. She will enjoy the freedom of not having to sell, or buy out, or share anything with her siblings. She used to dream of the Mediterranean, and often mentioned owning her own yacht. I wonder if she will ever make it come true. Knowing Suzanna, she will try hard enough. And Lewis will help her make it happen.

Umberto Ugobaldi will make the precise calculations, and tell me whether I have figured correctly whether the bank account I currently use, and my father's remaining investments, will – after succession duty is subtracted – cover the tax due on the entire legacy. In this way, neither house nor portfolio will have to be sold to pay for any state impost, and Paola, Suzanna, Brod and Nigel can enjoy their inheritance intact.

It was great fun to meet and talk with Matilde last week. Her niece Anna has arrived in Prato and is such a caring person. I know my old friend is now in good hands.

'What can I do for you?' Matilde kept asking me. I had to laugh. She was always so thoughtful and considerate. It was time I did something for her.

'But you paid us! You paid me and Donato, so well, too. Is there anything I can do for you … anything you need from Prato?'

So I told her what she could do. She could take several things off my hands as I decluttered the villa. The accumulated belongings of decades are not always sentimental. There were small appliances, rugs, kitchenware, stools and tools and more which would prove useful to her and others.

But there was another important task – to deliver to Paola, Suzanna, Brod, and Nigel the four little secret gifts I have planned for them. They are not bequests, strictly speaking, but giving them back objects from their childhood, objects which would always serve as memory triggers.

Memories – ah! They are not all good. Because of the way I am, I choose to isolate the good ones, and make much of those. There is enough bitterness and sorrow in life without demarcating negative recollections. The children must all have things to regret. With someone like Paola, they become plain on the face. With someone like Suzanna they are exclaimed over for a split second and quickly forgotten, or intentionally discarded. For Nigel, they become something to be sorted out with Harriet, darling Harriet – always another daughter to me. And Brod? Ah, Brod. He always brought his troubles to me. What will he do now?

Quiet, quiet. I should not shed tears for them. They are four fortunate people. More blessed than they know, with their strong personalities and all sorts of things they got from Roland.

They will most certainly have different memories ... depending on what made a lasting impression on each of their inquiring minds as they grew. So, as Matilde pointed out to me once, might very well remember the same events in very different ways.

What stirring events some of them were. How changed they always returned to the two houses from school each year. What attention I needed to pay to each little personality. How many individual pancake feasts I conjured up, to elicit from a youngster replete with blackberry juice and sugar the secrets, adventures, fears and desires of a maturing heart.

What fine times we had in Fiesole.

If you enjoyed this novel, please consider leaving your opinion as a review on Amazon.

You might enjoy another of this author's novels. See all Rosanne Dingli's fiction at

amazon.com/Rosanne-Dingli/e/B002BOJFCM

28628812R00155

Printed in Great Britain
by Amazon